Francis Charles Philips

A lucky young woman. A novel

Vol. I: A novel

Francis Charles Philips

A lucky young woman. A novel
Vol. I: A novel

ISBN/EAN: 9783743420069

Manufactured in Europe, USA, Canada, Australia, Japa

Cover: Foto ©Andreas Hilbeck / pixelio.de

Manufactured and distributed by brebook publishing software (www.brebook.com)

Francis Charles Philips

A lucky young woman. A novel

A LUCKY YOUNG WOMAN.

A Novel.

BY

F. C. PHILIPS,

AUTHOR OF "AS IN A LOOKING-GLASS."

IN THREE VOLUMES.
VOL. I.

London:

WARD AND DOWNEY,
12, YORK STREET, COVENT GARDEN.

1886.

A LUCKY YOUNG WOMAN.

CHAPTER I.

SIR HUGO CONYERS, the sixth baronet, ought to have been a very rich man. He ought to have been—so he would tell you at Boodles, as he sat in the window to put himself *en evidence* for the afternoon, before making his way to some cheap restaurant for his dinner—worth at least fifty thousand a year. The Conyers estates were in North Wales, and would no doubt have brought in Sir Hugo the amount he named had they

VOL. I.   B

been unencumbered.   But Sir Hugo's father
had been extravagant before him.

We need not tell the old story of cards
and racing and heavy betting.   When Sir
Hugo succeeded to the title every acre that
could be sold had gone, and he himself had
joined with his father in so heavily en-
cumbering what remained that his income
consisted of some few hundreds a year, which
were paid him quarterly by the trustees of
his mother's marriage settlement, and which
he could not possibly anticipate or get into his
hands in any way.   No solicitor in London
would advance him a farthing upon the
security of a property mortgaged up to the
hilt, and within two years after he succeeded his father the mortgagees foreclosed,
and Conyers Castle passed into the hands of
a rich iron-master and quarry-owner.

There remained for Sir Hugo the modest income we have already mentioned. Upon this he somehow just contrived to exist. He was at the time this story commences some fifty-five years of age, and had been a widower for ten years. The chief remaining trouble of his life—for he had grown callous, and some men who knew him went so far as to say shameless, about things that usually trouble or ought to trouble a gentleman if he have them, such as his tradesmen's accounts and his debts of honour—was his daughter Marcia, who was now nineteen.

In the first place, Sir Hugo did not care for his daughter in the least. She was an annoyance to him, and in an indolent, selfish kind of way he disliked her on that account. He would sometimes, indeed, as he drank

his glass of spirits and water in his bed-
room before retiring for the night, frame
a more or less definite wish, which went
rather beyond the mere expression of a
regret, that she had ever been born. But
apparently these paternal hopes were not
likely to be realized. Marcia was, as an
English girl of her age ought to be, the
picture of health, and Sir Hugo used to
finish his brandy and water and go to bed,
thinking over what might have been if
things had gone differently—a course of
meditation in which men who have reck-
lessly and wantonly thrown away their
chances and wasted their lives are very apt
to indulge, usually attributing the blame
to their own bad luck, or to a shameful
absence of any proper sense of duty on the
part of their friends and relations.

Marcia's mother when she became Lady
Conyers had immense expectations.   Her
father was one of those great monied men
who have become more and more a power
in the state since we were wicked enough
to repeal the Corn Laws, and to do other
things equally calculated to destroy our
old titled and landed families.

When Mr. Sandarson's daughter married
Sir Hugo he paid his son-in-law's debts
without any inquiry further than as to
their amount, and he also was liberal as a
rich father-in-law ought to be in the way
of an annual allowance ; but with all the
instincts of a man of business, he refused
to make any settlement upon his daughter,
contenting himself with the remark that his
name was sufficiently well known in the
City; that when he promised to pay so

much a-year he could pay it, and that when he died he should not forget his only daughter. As for his capital, he said he wanted it in his business, where it could make fifteen per cent. safely instead of being tied up at three and a half.

This was frank enough, and Sir Hugo was more than contented at the time with the three thousand a-year which her father's solicitors transmitted punctually to Lady Conyers, and with the certain prospect, as every one then supposed, that the old gentleman would die worth a sum so large that even Sir Hugo himself began to wonder at the possibilities of enjoyment that would be opened to him when his wife should succeed to her share of it. Meantime he reflected he could always get a little extra ready money out of his father-in-law at a pinch.

The pinches were frequent, and the old man, to do him justice, did not grumble at them more than was necessary and reasonable, especially when his daughter acted as mediator and peacemaker.

Commercial fortunes, however, are even more uncertain than are landed estates, and bankruptcy may come upon the one as suddenly and to the outer world as unexpectedly as a suit for foreclosure upon the other. The City one morning was struck with something like panic to hear that the great house of Sandarson had suspended payment, involving with it in its fall—so the rumour went—one or two large houses as well, and possibly even the bank which had been honoured with its account.

The rumour was correct except as regarded the bank, which had for some time past looked suspiciously at the paper of Sandarson and Company, and had at last flatly refused to discount that commodity at all without a margin so considerable that the refusal amounted virtually to a direct denial of what is known as ordinary mercantile credit.

Mr. Sandarson himself must have foreseen the crash for some time, and he did not survive it many months. Kindly people said he died of a broken heart. Those who suffered by his fall were less charitable, and declared that for years he had known what was coming, and instead of facing his difficulties, had to brace himself up from day to day with champagne and ultimately with brandy.

It matters little what people say of a man after he has failed in business, and nothing what they say of him when he is dead. Mr. Sandarson died before the full extent of his liabilities was known.

There was great sympathy felt for Sir Hugo in the sacred precincts of Boodles. Men of the fashionable world know, as a rule, that their most intimate friends are selfish and heartless. Very few if any of the members of Boodles had the slightest regard or even respect for Sir Hugo Conyers, but the heartlessness of his father-in-law, in having the presumption to fail for a sum of which even a small slice would have made most of them happy, wounded their moral susceptibilities very painfully.

" A man in business," profoundly observed an old gentleman, who, having spent his wife's fortune and his own, was now just able to keep his name on the books of the Club and pay his Club accounts and debts of honour by directing and promoting Joint Stock Companies, "a man of business has no business to fail. I consider Sandarson far worse than a defaulter. A horse may break its leg, or you may have a run of luck against you at piquet—even with the best play—but for a business man to fail is inexcusable. It shows that he does not understand what ought to be an absolute certainty."

In this opinion the bulk of the company seemed to concur. Some of them, indeed, openly avowed a strong opinion that Sir Hugo had been robbed by his father-in-law, while those who best knew the baronet himself discussed the interesting question how he would take it.

Sir Hugo took it as might have been
expected from a gentleman with his wide
knowledge of the world and peculiarly
philosophic temperament. He became so
careful over whist and *écarté*, and so successful when he took the trouble to form an
opinion on the merits of a horse, that many
of his old friends began to fight shy of him.
The limits of even the oldest friendship
are apt to become strained when the luck
invariably falls to Damon and not to
Pythias. And then, too, men who gamble
even within their means are apt to be un-
reasonable, and to say nasty things of those
to whom they habitually lose. So although
Sir Hugo kept his name on the books of
Boodles, he gave up frequenting the card-
room of that establishment, and contented
himself with the bow window in the after-

noon, where he would sit pretending to read the paper until his dinner hour, when he would descend the steps with an air so self-possessed that the oldest loungers in Clubland could hardly have made a guess at his destination and its object.

All these things make a man bitter in proportion to his selfishness. It galled Hugo Conyers to move about like one of Homer's ghosts in the world to which he had once belonged and to be denied its pleasures. To him the delights of Clubland were real and tangible—among the few things worth living for. He had just that amount of good taste which thoroughly selfish men about town acquire. He liked Boodles because it was old and select. He could appreciate its cookery and the vintages in its wine list. The butler respected his opinion and the chief valued his commendation. And Mr. Gainer himself would have allowed him much of that latitude which existed in the old days of the "account per contra at Brooks'," rather than see his name disappear from the list of members.

We need only add what the reader will probably have guessed for himself, that from the time of Mr. Sandarson's failure Sir Hugo persistently ill-treated his wife. When a British workman is out of employment, and cannot enjoy his usual allowance of beer and tobacco, he is apt to be indignant with his wife because she cannot set forth the dinner-table in its accustomed manner, and to evince his displeasure in a practical form by beating her. Sir Hugo Conyers could not beat his wife, but studied neglect and bitter words can be made more cruel than any blows; and of these Lady Conyers had more than even those who knew her husband and his disposition most thoroughly could ever have guessed. She lingered on for several years as only a woman can. She had hard work in their little house in Sloane Street to make both ends meet, and to keep her husband from open outbreaks of temper, but she toiled bravely. While Sir Hugo was at Boodles, or in the Park, or looking in at Tattersalls, of which he still continued a member, she would occupy herself with that domestic drudgery which is often an anodyne to women.

They kept but one maid in these days of famine, so Lady Conyers herself did much of the work of the house; and there was always her child, little Marcia. Marcia and her mother dined at one, and if the little girl had acquitted herself creditably in the morning over her spelling, she would be allowed to go out with her mother in the afternoon and look at the shops, or walk in the park.

Marcia's life was happy enough, for she was too young to understand or even guess at the things that had happened. She used to like to walk out with her mother or to sit with her at home. Poor Lady Conyers, who was devoted to the child, used to play the piano to her, and show her how to dress and undress her favourite doll, and to read stories to her and tell her fairy tales.

An only child will usually either turn out very well or very ill, and the happiest children are those who have brothers and sisters. Marcia showed signs of turning out well. She was obedient, docile, quick-witted, and extremely affectionate. It is impossible to expect more from a child of seven. It is very seldom that you get as much.

When they told her that her mother had gone away and was an angel in Heaven,—this was told her by the hospital nurse and by the servant, Heaven not lying within the range of Sir Hugo's ideas,—she had no more than a child's notion of what had really happened, and of all that she had lost. She suffered as children of her age do suffer when they lose a mother who has brought them up herself, and she for a long time refused comfort.

The daily governess, who was engaged

until, as Sir Hugo feelingly remarked, things had got into shape, did something to brighten the child's life. She was a German *fräulein* of the pleasantest type— and the Germans are kindly to children, and show their kindness for them in a practical way that children appreciate. German nursery tales and German toys are marvels not to be approached in their kind, and for a little girl left in the world without mother, brothers and sisters, or even playfellows, a kind-hearted German governess comes as a Providence that is sorely needed.

Fräulein Dietz was a kindly, simple, busy, cheerful little body, and soon had entirely won Marcia's heart. She showed her pupil pictures of all kinds, and told her what they represented when the letterpress offered difficulties. She began to teach her the piano, and gave her some idea of how she would have to play it when her hands were larger; and she also taught her to chatter fluently in German, and to pick her way through easy French lesson books.

I believe, indeed I am sure, that German governesses, like German professors, are the best of their kind. Teaching with them is not a means of livelihood so much as a pursuit which they thoroughly enjoy, and they make it their business to teach systematically and soundly. Nor do I agree with those who accuse them of faults of temper. On the contrary, I have always found the Teutonic temper to be fond of authority, but at the same time patient, gentle, and capable of great affection.

Marcia was a pupil whom, as a famous

Head Master once observed, it paid you to teach. She was also a child whom it was difficult not to love, so that when the first storm of her grief had calmed her days passed brightly and pleasantly with the warm-hearted, motherly Fräulein. They were the happiest days she was to know for many years to come.

Sir Hugo, finding that Fräulein Dietz was able to manage his little daughter so admirably, came to the conclusion that it would be wise on his part to retain her services altogether. And although the salary he offered was by no means a tempting one, yet the Fräulein, having become devotedly attached to her little charge, was fain to accept it, and henceforward she resided altogether in the house.

The Fräulein and Marcia had many little

pleasures of their own, and many little household matters upon their hands that made time glide by hour after hour and week after week almost unheeded. Upon the Fräulein, indeed, it seemed as if time could not possibly have any effect unless it might be to turn absolutely white hair that here and there already showed a silvery glint. She was the typical German woman, differing as much from all ordinary notions we entertain as to what a German Fräulein who bids fair to become an old maid may resemble, as does one of our own healthy English girls, whom you may see any day where girls are to be found,—in the Park, or on the Brighton Parade, or at Scarborough, or where you please,—from the marvellous *Mees Anglaise* portrayed by Cham in Charivari. How Leech, who could draw an English girl as truly as Landseer could paint deer or hound, must have laughed as he turned over Charivari at his Club.

Fräulein Dietz was short, of course, and also stout, with blue eyes and light hair, genuinely Teuton. Profane critics, who like the lean, colourless horrors sung by M. Rossetti and Mr. Swinburne, and painted by Mr. Paul Burne Jones, would have considered Miss Dietz, to use a plain English word, podgy. But there was a depth of honesty and affection in her blue eyes, and her heart was as simple as a child's and as tender as that of a mother. And qualities such as these will go far to counterbalance a carriage that is not altogether Parisian, and a Teutonic homeliness such as is sometimes supposed by people who knew everything to indicate want of education, or, as it pleases them to call it, culture.

Such, to sketch her briefly, was Fräulein Dietz, Marcia's second mother and constant companion. And it must be added, that the Fräulein had many other most estimable virtues. She was cheerful, industrious, bright, full of life, extremely affectionate, and absolutely devoid of selfishness.

It was little wonder that Marcia should love Fräulein Dietz, and that when Sir Hugo thought it time that the governess should return to Germany or seek out some other engagement, Marcia should be able to point out that the Fräulein was, in fact, housekeeper rather than ex-governess, and that it would be a very false economy indeed to lose her services, even although she herself was now nineteen.

"You see, papa," urged Marcia, "the Fräulein has taught me as much as she can make me learn; but she will never teach me to manage a house, or to keep the servants in order, or to look after those tiresome little bills which run away with more money than the big ones. She has tried very hard to do so, I know; but she laughs at me, and declares it isn't in me. Why, papa, if the Fräulein went away the servants would do exactly as they pleased, the tradesmen would cheat me shamefully, and our bills would be terrible."

Sir Hugo saw the force of this, and ungraciously gave his consent to the Fräulein's remaining. Whereat, I grieve to say, for the credit of Marcia's veracity, that she and the Fräulein laughed very heartily in

the evening over their little old-fashioned
repast of tea, toast, and watercress.

On the other hand, Sir Hugo consoled
himself with reflecting that the Fräulein's
salary was small, that he need not trouble
himself to pay it regularly, and that after
all it was probably cheaper to let her stop.
She cost little more than a servant, and no
doubt Marcia was right in contending that
she saved that little two or three times
over; and with these calculations Sir Hugo
consoled himself as he sat in his easy-chair
at Boodles, and remembering dimly and
wistfully how he had always wished to live,
and pondering gloomily upon the shabby
way in which fortune had treated him.

"It is always so, sir," he said to himself.
"It is only the snobs who have a chance
in these days, even in the service.   Fellows

who can live and dress themselves on a hundred a year." Which course of reflection led him to the conclusion that the country was going to the devil, and that he could not do better than fortify himself with a stiff glass of brandy and water.

CHAPTER II.

SIR HUGO was, as I have said, fifty-five years of age. He did not attempt to conceal this fact, as it stood on record in Burke and Debrett. You must not contradict things that are written in the book of Jasher, or when your back is turned, some young gentleman may despatch the smoking-room waiter for the awkward record and turn you into ridicule. So Sir Hugo never alluded to his age, but carried it pleasantly and, indeed, almost defiantly. And to do him justice, he was very well preserved.

Time does not tell upon men who are idle and self-indulgent, unless they also have a bad constitution or lead a vicious life. Now Sir Hugo's constitution was apparently excellent. His teeth were sound, and his digestion unimpaired. He walked erectly, and had never been troubled with gout even in its premonitory form of indigestion. He was constitutionally lazy. He had never cared much even when young for tramping the stubbles or keeping well in the first flight; but during the few years that he was in the Guards he used to be considered a smart officer, and he still retained the dignity of his old military bearing without its stiffness.

Sir Hugo could not afford a valet, but he did not need one; and as you saw him make his way along Piccadilly and down

St. James's Street, you would think, not
knowing at whom you were looking, what
a fine, gallant, upright English gentleman
he was.

And indeed a man can preserve himself
wonderfully if he avoids vulgar vices, such
as indulgence in early drinks, or in the
still more fatal habit of eating more than he
requires; if he keeps regular hours; and if,
to use a comprehensive phrase, he takes
care of himself. Now Sir Hugo took care
of himself without being aware that he did
so, and consequently his years sat graciously
on him. Above all, he never troubled himself with thinking—a bad habit, tending
greatly to shorten our enjoyment of the
little span of life which the fates allow us.

It has been maliciously said, probably
by some ill-educated and ill-mannered non-

conformist, that deans live to an immense age, because they have a certain income, nothing to do for it, and a thoroughly comfortable deanery in which to do that nothing in a manner that becomes the environment and is worthy of it.

Sir Hugo, had he gone into the Church instead of into the Guards, would certainly have become a dean. And it is almost equally certain that in these later and vexatious days of ours, he would have refused a bishopric. And herein he would have been wise. Indeed, I, for my own humble part, would far sooner be Dean of Westminster than Archbishop of York, or even Canterbury.

It is difficult to describe Marcia Conyers. She was tall and upright like her father, with a head such as the old masters loved to paint, well poised upon a neck worthy of its burden. Her features were Roman rather than Greek, and her thick soft hair was of that deep black which, as the light glints upon it, seems to take a bluish tinge. Her eyes were of a colour that is rare—a deep iron brown, like that (if the comparison may be permitted) of a thoroughly tempered gun-barrel, and as fearless and resolute as those of a hawk. Her gait was not that now considered fashionable, nor was it that which the drill-master sometimes contrives to impart to tall young ladies as a last boarding-school touch. Perhaps I may best describe her by saying that the more plainly she dressed the more likely would she be to strike your attention. She was, indeed, as Tennyson has it in his vision of fair women—

"A daughter of the gods, divinely tall,
And most divinely fair."

It need only be added that she had admirably good taste and a faultless eye for colour, and that, as it can hardly be said she went into society, she dressed to please herself.

Now as Hugo Conyers was one day walking leisurely up Piccadilly he saw on the other side of the way, under the blank wall of Devonshire House, two ladies going in the direction of Knightsbridge, who were in fact his own daughter and Fräulein Dietz. It may seem odd that a man should not recognize his own daughter on the other side of the street, but as a matter of fact, Sir Hugo did not at first recognize Marcia.

Being too well-bred a gentleman to stare at a lady, he might have passed on with some vague wishes that he was still young and could begin life again, had not Marcia stopped and looked at him across the road. An uneasy suspicion at once flashed through his mind that she might want half a sovereign for further purchases, so he waved his hand with an air of dignified affection that spoke volumes. "Do not trouble to cross the road, my sweet child," that wave said; "I require nothing. God bless you. I am proud of you. You amply repay many years of toil and anxiety and self-denial." It was the gesture of a man who, like Lord Beaconsfield's Dukes in Lothair, thanks Providence devoutly that his children are not unworthy of him.

But as he made his way down St. James's Street towards Boodles other ideas came crowding into his head; and when he reached that club, and had ensconced himself in a comfortable arm-chair, he began to think so very seriously that many of the men in the room inclined to the opinion he must have lost money, while those who knew better favoured the idea that he had come into money, and was perhaps a little bewildered by it.

It was late enough in the year for a fire, and Sir Hugo sat before the fire and meditated. He also did what for him was an unusual thing; for when he had apparently finished his meditations he repaired to the coffee-room, where he very slowly and sedately, as becomes a gentleman of his age and position, recruited himself with a brown bread biscuit and two or three glasses of Madeira. Madeira was a wine he rarely touched, but on this occasion he felt a stimulant necessary, so he took his Madeira slowly, and, as it were, medicinally. When it was finished he repaired to the writing-room, and there, after making a careful draft with alterations, copied and despatched the following letter :—

"DEAR LADY ST. AUSTELL,

"I am going to presume upon our long friendship to ask a favour so slight that you need no more hesitate at its refusal than I at the suggestion.

"I know that at this time of the year your house is always full, but if you could make room for my daughter Marcia for a few days, I should be glad if you would let me send her.

"She has not lately been looking well. Of course she pretends that there is

nothing the matter with her, but I believe
the truth to be that the dear child fancies
I prefer Town myself even at this time of
year, and is unwilling to leave me.

"The air of Oakshire would, I am sure,
brace her wonderfully. As she has never
had a maid of her own she will, of course,
not bring one with her, but will not
encroach upon the time of yours.

"You will find her greatly grown.
Indeed I sometimes fear she has a little
out-grown her strength.

"About yourself, who have the gift of
perpetual youth, I need hardly ask. And
as I read in last Saturday's *Field* a full
account of the day in your coverts, I
know that St. Austell must be as vigorous
and hearty as ever.

"For myself, the days of gun and

D 2

saddle are gone; but age brings with it its own consolations and even its own enjoyments.

"Pray answer this letter as frankly as I hope I have written it. If you are full I shall take Marcia down to Brighton, which is now and long has been my country residence.

"Remember me most kindly to St. Austell, and believe me,

"Ever sincerely yours,

"Hugo Conyers."

The composition of this letter took some little time, and when it was finished and despatched, Sir Hugo, with the proud feeling that he was a father who did his duty at any denial or sacrifice to himself, ordered a dinner which he felt he had thoroughly

earned—half-a-dozen oysters, a little clear
soup, a partridge, and some caviare on toast,
and to this, with an Imperial pint of champagne, he did ample justice.

He felt that he had done his duty to his
daughter, and deserved a dinner a little out
of the common as its reward. He did not
read after dinner, for he took care of his
eyes, as of all other things essential to his
own comfort and enjoyment, but he sat
over the table for some little time with a
small cup of black coffee.

Sir Hugo was just about to leave the
club, when a sudden thought occurred to
him. He turned into the morning-room
and took up the *Morning Post*.

There he read as follows :—

"The Earl and Countess of St. Austell
are entertaining a small circle of friends at

St. Austell Towers, Oakshire, including the Austrio-Hungarian Ambassador and the Countess Olmutski, the Duke and Duchess of Lincoln, the Earl of Norwich, the Earl and Countess of Deepdale, and the ladies Gwendoline and Isabel Austice, Sir Michael Govett, Sir George and Lady Heythrop and Miss Heythrop, Colonel Hewland, Royal Horse Guards, the Honourable and Reverend Sidney Winthrop, Mr. and the Honourable Mrs. Carpenter, Major Allardyce, Mr. Davidson, M.P. &c."

"I could not possibly have done better," said Sir Hugo to himself, as he stood on the mat while the porter hailed a cab, a comfort to which this excellent parent felt himself fully entitled after his day's work. "It looks almost like the finger of Providence."

The cabman on being paid his exact fare at the door in Sloane Street took a different view of Providence and its workings, in which two other cabmen, whom he met at the Cadogan Arms, where he assuaged his anger with rum and shrub, fully concurred.

"That's where it is in a club," observed one of these two philosophers. " If you're in the street and off the rank you can pick your man. Get called to a club and you never know what to expect. And what I say is this—the sweller the club the meaner the man. Ah! nine times out of ten."

Sir Hugo for once in a way was not discontented after his fashion or in his own heart with the ways of Providence, and went to bed with a misty sort of idea that to be a good parent is its own reward.

This took more definite shape as he fell asleep, thinking of Marcia's age, and of other things, all of which would have been pleasant enough were it not for the reflection that she would need one or two new dresses at least, and that she had no credit running with any West End milliner.

"After all," he thought, "the girl always looks at her best in her plainest dress. I think I ought to know. And as there are other girls there they will act as a foil to her. In plain muslin and black ribbon, or cherry,—yes, cherry for choice, —I'd back her against most fields she is likely to meet."

Excellent meditations such as these soon had their effect, and Sir Hugo fell into that peaceful sleep which ought always to follow a day that has been conscientiously devoted to hard work for a worthy object.

* * * * *

By the earliest possible post Sir Hugo received from Lady St. Austell the most gracious of answers. Lady St. Austell would be delighted if Marcia would come down at once, and stop as long as she pleased. Would not Sir Hugo come down too? Of course the men were all busy in the truly English pastime of killing something. Day after day it was either hunting or shooting, so that nothing was seen of them until dinner-time, after which they retired to the smoking-room and went religiously to sleep. But Sir Hugo could please himself, and might stop indoors all day, and give Lady St. Austell and her friends the pleasure of his society. If, on the other hand, he found the air of Oak-shire suit him, he could amuse him as he pleased. There were horses that wanted both riding and driving, and the grounds, for the time of the year, were really in capital order. She need not add that her house was Liberty Hall, and that in all that he did or left undone he could conduct himself exactly as if he was in his own house.

Sir Hugo's reply did not take him long. He had many reasons for accepting the invitation, and none for refusing it. He felt that for himself a change would do him good, and would even be an economy, after all incidental expenses (including tips) had been reckoned up to a five-shilling-piece; and in his own case there would be no tips to huntsmen, whips, or keepers—

heavy items, as many a young man has had cause to know.

Sir Hugo sent one of his most courtly replies, and two days later was on his way with Marcia to St. Austell Towers.

The journey down, although as a rule he hated railway journeys, actually seemed to invigorate Sir Hugo. He talked cheerfully to Marcia about his own exploits in earlier days with the gun and across country, and he actually went so far as to declare that had he only a decent place of his own in the country, no power on earth should tempt him up to London, unless it were for something really important, such as to be present at Court on Marcia's introduction.

He became, indeed, so amiable that Marcia was almost bewildered, and marvelled whether she might have come across some

" streak," as the Americans call it, in her
father, the existence of which she had not
as yet even suspected. And when they
were met by an open carriage—for it was a
bright sunny day—and were being whirled
along the road by a pair of sturdy, fast-
going horses, she almost forgot all first
disagreeables in the exhilaration which fresh
air, fair English scenery, rapid motion, and
a clear sky will produce even in the most
confirmed invalid, but which in the young
is a something as indescribable as the effect
of good champagne taken in reason and at
the right time.

Everything was new to this London girl
who knew but little, indeed nothing, of our
most beautiful English scenery, except from
the Academy and from Vernon Heath's
photographs.

Marcia would have clapped her hands with pleasure had she been alone at the mere sight of the hedgerows,— always picturesque,—and of the cattle, and the quaint cottages in the old village, and the little stream with a bridge that seemed almost an artificial ruin, it so invited the sketcher by its infinite variety of dilapidation and tint.

And then, as the gates were swung open, they entered the park and dashed through an avenue such as England only can boast. On each side were the great elms; and under the oaks away in the turf the deer were busy among the fallen acorns, and the carriage wheels startled a great jay, all chocolate and lapis lazuli, who scuttered away with his own shriek of anger and noisy complaint at being disturbed.

Nor was this all, for a little stone bridge took them over the stream which fed the lake, where there were swans both black and white, and as many other kinds of water-fowl as even St. James's Park had ever shown her in her morning walks. And there was the home farm, with its little herd of cattle, and its goats, and a large enclosure for some kangaroos. And then they came to thick shrubberies carefully planted with evergreens, until the coachman checked his horses to an inch at the door of an English house such as it is a pleasure even to look at through a railway window.

For The Towers were an old red-brick Tudor mansion which might, before the time of heavy guns, have almost stood a siege. The moat round it had been drained, and its sides laid out as terraces, which in summer were bright with flowers. The windows had been fitted with modern sashes and plate glass, and in the centre of the quadrangle, which could easily have held two or three troops of horse, a fountain now leaped into the air, which in warm weather fell upon centenarian gold fish basking among broad water-lily leaves, but now threw a crystal jet in the spray of which the bright sun painted a glorious rainbow.

Round all four sides of the court ran a genuine cloister, the roof of which formed a terrace and summer garden to the first floor. Over the gateway was the clock tower. Wolsey might have built St. Austell Towers as a summer pleasaunce for himself while meditating Hampton Court.

At the doorway Sir Hugo and Marcia

were received with due solemnity by a hall
porter, who must have been some close
relation of that colossal and impenetrable
marvel of his kind who did duty at North-
umberland House before its demolition, and
from whom they gathered that his lordship
and the party had not returned from the
coverts, and that her ladyship had driven
over to the town.

After imparting this information he
touched some electric bells, a footman and
a ladies' maid appeared upon the scene, and
Marcia found herself in a chamber looking
out upon the park with its deer, and the
like of which she had never seen before.
For it was a large oak-panelled room, with
a great stone window, and a ceiling painted
by Verrio. But the furniture was entirely
modern, with the one exception of the fire-

place, which had an immense carved mantel-piece. Under this, in a recess of Dutch tiles, had been fitted, perhaps by way of contrast, the brightest and most cheerful of little grates; and on the top of the coals billets of pine were sputtering and crackling a welcome, and throwing fitful lights and shadows on the old oak and on some Lelys and Vandycks for which the galleries had not room.

It was pleasant to learn that there were still three hours before dinner, and I believe that young ladies after a long railway journey and a brisk drive in cold weather enjoy tea and hot dry toast as much as Sir Hugo himself was at that moment luxuriating in a glass of brandy and water and a rusk with some devilled caviare.

CHAPTER III.

PAPER Buildings in the Temple are
strangely altered from what they once were.
If you doubt this, make your way to the
Inner Temple Library, the courteous libra-
rian of which noble collection will, after
duly verifying your credentials, place at
your disposal a rare portfolio of old steel
engravings and other treasures dating from
the days when Ben Jonson wrote masques
to be played before Queen Elizabeth in
the Middle Temple Hall, and her Majesty
showed her appreciation of the entertain-
ment by ordering that the noble chamber

should be newly panelled with oak from the wreck of the Armada, down to these later times of the Law Almanack, in which, when the Benchers of an Inn of Court determine to spend their money lest a Radical Government should lay plundering hands upon it, they exhaust their treasure-chest and mortgage the credit of the Inn to erect piles of stone such as the pepper-potted building on the Embankment, which in my own humble opinion must have been built from designs originally intended for a grand hotel at a new and rising watering-place, and which has hardly its equal in London for ugliness. Paper Buildings are now almost entirely occupied by men in active and busy practice, and in term time the stairs are beset with passengers, from the Queen's Counsel or Junior hurrying

across to the Law Courts, down to the
solicitor's clerk or errand-boy, with a brief
to be delivered or a consultation to be
fixed.

John Douglas had his business chambers
on the ground-floor in one of these dull
stone buildings, and herein he showed
his wisdom; for although the first floor
is affected by Queen's Counsel and even
by Juniors in heavy mercantile practice
(which they usually owe to private interest),
solicitors have a weakness for the ground-
floor, as it saves them the trouble of
mounting and again descending a cold
stone staircase, trying to the limbs and
temper of elderly gentlemen in comfortable
circumstances.

But Mr. Douglas' residential chambers
were in King's Bench Walk, upon the

second floor, and of these few except his clerk knew the secret; for he was a methodical man, who liked to keep the hours of business absolutely apart from those of rest. His career had not been exactly brilliant. He had not rowed in the University eight, or carried off the Newdigate, or done any other of those things which are considered "crack" successes. He had been at Harrow, where he was in the eleven, had proceeded from Harrow to Baliol, where he took a first-class of the kind that is called "solid," rowed in the college eight because he said he wanted exercise, but declined the honour of representing his University at Putney, and left Oxford without a Fellowship, because he had inherited a few hundreds a year from his father, which disqualified him as a candidate anywhere but at St. Asaph's—a corporate body to which he did not aspire to belong. He came to the Bar, and here again worked steadily and with method.

If you do this and wait your time your chance is sure to come, and Douglas' chance came soon. It was no single event, such as the one speech which made the fortune of Erskine. It consisted of a series of small successes which gradually brought him into notice, so that one day, when a gentleman who had for thirty years been standing Counsel to the Kettle-Makers' Company, and half-a-dozen other City guilds, to say nothing of banks and firms, was raised to the Bench, the bulk of his business gravitated naturally to Douglas, who, as a matter of fact, now counted his income in four figures, of which the first was not a unit.

His tastes were simple, and he could afford to gratify them, and yet live very considerably within his income. He belonged to the Oxford and Cambridge, he had a small yacht of thirty tons in Dover harbour, as being of easy access from London, and in the winter hunting and shooting were always ready for him, as he was a capital guest in a country-house, and far too much a man of the world to promote small jealousies by showing the residents the way over a fence, or wiping the eye of his neighbour over a bird.

Douglas was a little over thirty-five years of age, tall, upright, and well set together, with broad shoulders and a deep chest. Perhaps few women would have considered him handsome. Suffice it to say, that he had dark brown hair which curled crisply, keen grey eyes, a sunburnt complexion, and features which were strongly marked.

Men, indeed, who did not like him used to declare that he resembled Lord Combermere, Wellington's favourite general of cavalry. I have noticed, by the way, that strongly-marked features are seen to advantage under a white wig, and assist a young barrister more than might be generally supposed in his professional career. Douglas was at this moment, the last few weeks of the long vacation, at St. Austell Towers, whither batches of what are called "papers" used to come down to him from town.

A man of strong constitution can get through a considerable amount of work whilst staying at a country-house without in any way appearing to withdraw himself from its society ; and, indeed, if you do not need to be constantly consulting a library of reference, the amount of work through which you can get in a limited time under the stimulus of country air is astonishing.

Now Sir Hugo had never so much as heard the name of John Douglas, for he never looked at the Law Reports in the *Times*, unless it were to glance at a murder trial, or a piquant divorce case, or a jewel robbery of more than general interest. He had a vague idea that young barristers lived somewhere under the tiles in Pump Court, and made their breakfast off a red-herring toasted for them by an Irish laundress.

How some few of them emerged from this obscurity to become judges, or even

to occupy the woolsack, was a problem he
had never considered. Indeed, of the Bar
and of men at the Bar he knew about as
much as can be learnt about her Majesty's
services from reading Marryat's sea stories
and Lever's novels, in which we gather
only one side of the life usually led by
the Queen's officers, forgetting other sides
such as those shown us in Wellington's
despatches.

This kind of ignorance is far more
general than might be fancied, even by
men who live in what is called the
world. And it is perhaps some excuse
for Sir Hugo that John Douglas was
not yet in Parliament. A seat in the
House of Commons is not always a prize
which a barrister of eminence need covet,
and has long ceased to be in itself a

short road to the Bench. Consequently, Douglas had not attempted to get into the House, having indeed other things to do.

But he was known, as I have said, to the great mercantile firms in the City, and the judges listened to his arguments with attention, knowing that he never took untenable points, or wasted their time by talking to please his clients. In court, in fact, as in the hunting-field, he took his own line; and I have noticed that judges are very like masters of fox-hounds, in one respect at any rate—that they can soon see whether a man is up to his work, and has the right stuff in him.

A barrister in large practice has hardly time to dine out, and certainly none for balls or receptions. He consequently escapes those opportunities of falling in love which offer themselves so freely to gentlemen who have nothing to do after four in the afternoon, and very often nothing to do until noon the next day, unless they choose to mark themselves by excess of zeal, which in her Majesty's Civil Service, at any rate, is by no means the certain road to promotion that might be supposed.

When John Douglas was in London his habits were as methodical as those of a clock. He rose early, had his breakfast at once, and then took a brisk walk or a sharp three quarters of an hour in the saddle.

If you are in large practice you must be ready for consultation by nine in the morning. Court will take you the whole day. The Court risen, you will have other consultations until seven or thereabouts. Then if you are wise, as John Douglas was, you will dine at your club, play a game or two at billiards, or join in a rubber, and be in bed as early as possible.

It may be asked how it is that barristers at the head of their profession ever manage to read their briefs. The thing seems at first impossible. And yet we know that it is done. First there is the simple explanation that they are clear-headed men, who get through their work rapidly and yet thoroughly, so that one reading of a case is all they want. Then, too, there is a certain method of compassing their work which they somehow acquire. This is not a secret known to the bulk of the profession, and it is the men that possess it who come to the front. Besides, one case is very like another, and the more you practise at the Bar the more law you learn. It is not the men who write law books and compile digests that get into leading practice, however sound may be their written opinions.

Law, indeed, is in this respect exactly like its sister learned profession, medicine. The men who are deservedly most eminent in it have no time to read, much less to write. They have an experience and knowledge greater than that of books, and are always in advance of the books which are at the time the standard authorities.

It may almost be said of them that they make law and medicine for the next generation, and have no occasion to study either the law or the medicine of the past.

CHAPTER IV.

THE drawing-room at St. Austell Towers was a curious mixture of old, new, and antique, and yet in perfect taste. The oak panelling still remained, but had upon it, hung low and within view, late pictures by modern artists. Above these were mirrors of Venetian glass, with countless tapers that threw quaint many-hued lights. The furniture was in character with the room. There were cabinets, some Louis Quatorze with priceless *plaques* of porcelain; some of deeply-carved teak and ebony from Burmah, with grotesque and hideous figures

on them deeply cut; others of old oak
found in hidden Dutch towns and villages,
and each was loaded with china Oriental
and European, with Indian work of silver
spun out into cobwebs, and with things
even rarer than these, such as bowls cut
without flaw from a single block of
rock crystal; and as counter-marvels of
mechanical skill, cunning toys which had
taken years in their construction.

A Chinaman, it has been said, will spend
ten years of his life in saving the money
with which to buy the root of a great
elephant tusk. Out of this he will cut a
spherical ball, through the holes of which
you see another ball, and through those
yet another, until the sphere inside com-
pletes the magic number of even fifty.

Burmese lacquer boxes, the largest the

size of a tea-caddy, the smallest and inner-most less than a hazel nut, and silver boxes from the Hague, out of which, when you touched a spring, started a tiny humming-bird, round which a lady could put her ring, flapped his wings, flirted his tail, vibrated his little beak, trilled a song, and so retired again with a snap into his box.

It was a museum rather than a room had you chosen to spend a couple of days in it. And, on the other hand, there were signs of modern life. For Lord St. Austell, like many other men of unlimited wealth, had also good taste, and everywhere about were vases of exquisite hot-house blossoms; for the sake of which the head-gardener had a joint control over the chamber with the housekeeper, carefully regulating the temperature and taking a pride in his work.

Marcia was not bewildered by this marvellous display. She would have liked, no doubt, a couple of days to herself—a week would not really have been too much—to go through the room leisurely, as if it were a museum. This, however, was a pleasure that might well wait for the first rainy day, which would probably be to-morrow or the day after, two fine days in succession in October being a feat of which our climate is, as a rule, incapable.

So Marcia did as most young ladies do in the vexatious quarter of an hour that precedes dinner—that is to say, she took a seat (on an ottoman covered with rugs of the silver fox), and waited the turn of events.

Presently, of course, was heard a gong beaten in the most approved fashion, one that would puzzle the most accomplished drum-major in the British Army, and known to few but Burmese and the Chinamen of the Yellow River.

And so came dinner, and Marcia found herself on the arm of John Douglas, whom Lady St. Austell had just presented to her, and to whose charge her hostess had confided her. The staircase was as marvellous after its kind as the room they had left, and was panelled and decorated to match the dining-room, to which latter apartment, in my humble opinion, every staircase should be assimilated in manner and effect.

And in the dining-room again was black oak, from which the light of the wax

tapers glinted back, and above the oak, as
on the walls of the staircase and in the
hall, were trophies of the chase, and armour
and weapons of almost every age and
country, from chain mail of the crusaders
down to steel breast-plates worn by Crom-
well's Ironsides ; from pikes and matchlocks,
yataghans and krises, to relics of Waterloo,
the Crimea, and the Mutiny. But on the
table, with the exception of some rare old
silver and china that did duty in the
centre, all was modern, down even to the
menu daintily written in a little pasteboard
volume, which contained for the ladies
other trifles, such as a miniature looking-
glass and a button-hook for gloves.

Nor need I after this speak of the dinner
itself. Any man can give a good dinner
if he will give his mind to the task, and

the dinner will not be the worse if he can afford rarities.

Lord St. Austell had a good cook and a good butler. He regarded the day's dinner as one of the responsibilities attaching to his wealth, and a duty, or rather a courtesy, due to his guests. In this view his *chef*, his butler, and his head-gardener fully concurred. A dinner at such a table is not a thing to be forgotten. Marcia, ignorant of the difference between *bisque d'écrevisse* and *tortue claire*, and who had never seen in her life red mullet or lamprey, capercailzie or woodcock, except to wonder at them in shops, was fairly bewildered, and had to choose between refusing every dish offered to her, or, in the true spirit of a picnic, accepting the advice of John Douglas, who had the tact to perceive her trouble and the dexterity to help her through it without making her aware of the fact.

On Marcia's right hand was the old Duke of Lincoln, who cared for nothing in the world but pedigree cattle and subsoil drainage, and who consequently, relying on the strength of his title, took his dinner methodically, as becomes a Duke who owns one shire in the grazing counties and half another; and if he had known his Horace, whose very name he had forgotten since he was last flogged at Eton, might perhaps have thought of the ode in the first book, but who wisely contented himself with saying nothing.

On the left Douglas helped her through every difficulty; and here let me own at once, that I care very little for a

man who does not carry on well into
middle life and past it the heart and
feelings of five-and-twenty. Your cynics
of thirty are humbugs, bred of the tinpot
renaissance we owe to three distinguished
young gentlemen, and without the infinite
power of small talk which makes the
lesser followers of these luminaries entertaining even during the solemn period of
dinner. John Douglas was genuine, and
so he tried to find out what the girl he
had taken down to dinner might care to
talk about. If you once strike the true
note in a conversation everything will
follow smoothly, whether you are at a
dinner table, or in a railway train.

Douglas at a shot began with the flowers
in front of him. This led to a discussion
upon orchids, and Darwin, whom Marcia

happened to have read, and orchid-hunting
in tropical forests, and the risks and dangers
of orchid-hunters—a class of toilers of
whose very existence Marcia was ignorant,
having only a vague idea that orchids
came from the Brazils. And so the
minutes slipped by pleasantly enough for
Marcia.

A girl's first ball has had things before
it in her life that lead up to it. She has
been to archery meetings and other such
gatherings. But her first dinner-party is
an event in her life, and one which few
girls forget, even though it may have
fatigued and bored them.

In the drawing-room Marcia, by this time
thawed, began to feel thoroughly comfortable, if not indeed entirely happy. As
she had not in any way made herself re-

markable at dinner there was no set made upon her, and it was a novelty again to be in such a huge room, and to drink tea out of Dresden porcelain, and to play with biscuits, marvels of French manufacture, and to be able now at her leisure to wonder at the room and all that it contained.

And so she sat, still thinking more or less dreamily of everything and nothing, until she noticed that the men were coming up. The coffee did not take long. Most of the men were anxious to get to the smoking-room with its unholy comforts, and most of the ladies were equally anxious to get away. There are many reasons for this, of which I will give some in detail, as they have been imparted to me under terrible vows of secrecy.

In the first place, a good dress must not be worn too long at a time, and even muslin will show signs of wear sooner than might be expected from so simple and apparently innocent a fabric. I have heard, indeed, that a muslin dress must be—I hope my technical terms are correct —"unripped" and "done up" and put together again after its third evening of duty. Silk dresses are a mystery, of the proper management of which I know rather less than do the ladies who wear them of spot pool, or badger drawing, or boxing the compass. Secondly, the men themselves are believed to hold meetings in what is called the bachelors' room, where the butler makes his appearance with the butler's tray, containing curries and anchovy toast, and other such things, while his assistant brings up the rear with cigars and strong waters. And thirdly, as the men like the smoking-room, and often occupy it to an hour conventionally un-seasonable, so do the ladies congregate in the bed-room of some recognized leader. These be mysteries of the Bona Dea, and I shun the unenviable reputation of Clodius.

But I know that tea taken immediately before bed upsets the nerves and produces sleeplessness unless it be qualified, and that, with the aid of a dainty silver tea-kettle and its proper adjuncts, a scale of drinks can be concocted, commencing with hot port wine and water and ending with just that amount of cognac which doctors who know their profession are all agreed is often necessary after a tiring day for a married lady, and occasionally advisable,

under her permission, and if mixed by
herself, for even unmarried ladies who, after
the day's excitement, are feeling a peg too
low, and need a sound night's rest to
restore the roses to their cheek · next
morning.

The whole thing was new to Marcia.
She did not understand the things she
heard talked about, and consequently could
not even affect an interest in them.   Lady
St. Austell had deserted her, not unkindly
but entirely, to talk local politics to the
Duchess of Lincoln, and so it was a real
relief to her to find herself at last in
her own room, with the billets still blazing
and a sofa drawn before the fire, as if to
allure you into sitting up all night.   This
temptation—and I for my own part know
of none more insidious—Marcia resisted

stoutly; and was almost immediately asleep covered by and hidden in that mass of quilts and furs which you seldom see south of the Tweed, but on which a Scotch house prides itself.

And now I must say a word for John Douglas. This bad young man, whose failings it would be untruthful in me to extenuate, was among the last who sought their quarters in the bachelors' wing, where at St. Austell Towers license reigned without restriction. As I want my readers to know him thoroughly, they shall hear exactly what he did.

He was a methodical young man, so he hung up his dress clothes, spreading them wide, and sprinkling them with eau de cologne that they might be freed from the taint of the smoking-room. Then he

ensconced himself in an easy-chair and
lit a briar-wood pipe, moistening it with
some Athol-brose which the butler had
specially recommended.

Athol-brose is made in this wise. Upon
virgin honeycombs you pour, according to
their amount, the oldest French brandy
and the most indisputable Scotch whiskey
in equal proportions. You allow this
goodly mixture to stand for days in a large
pipkin, and in a cool place, and it is then
strained and ready for drinking. Epicures
drop into the jug by way of imparting
artistic finish a small fragment of the
honeycomb itself. This I deprecate. But
I can conscientiously aver that Athol-brose,
whether as first brewed by the butler or
whether after diluted by a cautious young
Englishman, is a beverage which, judiciously

taken, might well have comforted even Job in his most trying moments.

To a landsman after a day in the open air Athol-brose is in its sense as precious as egg-flip to the dwellers in the forecastle. Like egg-flip also, it makes you first contented, then retrospective, and finally drowsy, so that when he had finished his tumbler Douglas turned into bed with that peculiar feeling of delight which comes upon young men when they finish a well-spent day, and oddly enough began to think of his companion at the dinner-table, and to wonder where and how she had been brought up, and even to conjecture whether she was possibly thinking of himself. This last was very foolish on his part, for I am assured on the best authority that bed with young ladies is an institution too sacred to be disturbed by thought,—nay, more, that they fall asleep immediately, and resent being awakened in the morning.

If this be indeed true it is very sad, for it destroys our faith in all the pretty stories about St. Agnes' Eve and so on. But we must not inquire too deeply into certain secrets, and we may be quite sure in any case of this, if a young lady goes to bed with her mind half made up in the evening, she will wake up with it fully made up in the morning, for sleep, like old age, of which the ancients called it the precursor, only strengthens our convictions; and the wise man who told us not to let the sun go down upon our wrath judged well, whereas he who said "Think over it before you go to sleep," has been responsible for infinite mischief. A man is never so selfish as when he is falling asleep and the drowsiness of his body begins to creep to his mind.

Let us do John Douglas justice. He rose early next morning and, to use an intelligible phrase among young men, "shovelled on" a thick suit, in which he took a brisk walk of an hour and a half through interminable shrubberies, returning to his toilet with a swinging step, a clear head, and his mind made up, as he thought—wherein he deluded himself—that he would make up his mind very carefully within the next few days. And this is a dangerous attitude, and one into which a young man should never allow himself to be betrayed, for whereas when his seniors think over matters they usually end by the philosophic determination to do nothing, the young man who allows himself to think things over is almost certain to end by finding that he has done a great deal more than he ever intended.

You may illustrate this, if you have had the experience, by asking the value of your comparative chance from a young man and an old, when you have requested each to do you a good turn, and each has told you that he will think it over and let you know to-morrow, by which time he shall have made up his mind.

CHAPTER V.

BREAKFAST that morning was the desultory meal that it usually is in a large country-house. Marcia having ascertained that Lady St. Austell would not be down until ten, deferred her own appearance to that hour. Sir Hugo before descending fortified himself for the discharge of his paternal duties through the day with a brandy and soda, feeling that he had important business upon hand, and might really for once in a way, and under the influence of bracing country air, allow him-

G 2

self that gentle stimulant, with some dry toast as a sort of excuse.

It was nearly half-past eleven before Sir Hugo made his appearance at the breakfast table, to find that the men had all left for the coverts. There were, however, some few of the ladies scattered at the table, and Sir Hugo liked ladies' society as many thoroughly selfish men do. So he set to work, with the appetite of a Roman father, resolved to keep up his system, and in this respect acquitted himself very creditably.

Breakfast in a well-appointed country-house is a meal of delightful variety, a meal to think over and to enjoy leisurely. Young men do themselves lasting injury with mutton chops and strong coffee, and pressed beef and even ale. Sir Hugo had reached an age at which you know better, and at which you have learned to take care of yourself, and to regard a meal as a sort of duty which you owe to society. For men such as Sir Hugo know themselves and their own value, and are Cornaros upon a small scale, although, unless they are confirmed dyspeptics, they like a well-appointed table for its own sake, however moderately they may indulge their infinite field for choice. So Sir Hugo thoroughly enjoyed his cold partridge and hot tea, and felt so much the better for it as to follow the advice of the butler when that august official suggested, rather than recommended, green curaçon.

Green curaçon is said by many persons to be almost as poisonous as kirschenwasser, which contains I do not know how much per cent. of prussic acid. So does one of

Benson's big regalias contain enough nico-
tine to kill almost any animal of which I
know except a goat.   But exactly as some
young men find that a big cigar steadies
their nerves, so do many of their elders
derive comfort from prussic acid, which,
judiciously taken, is as valuable an item as
any in the pharmacopœia.

Breakfast over Sir Hugo felt some few
years younger, and began to seriously consider the business he had in hand.   It was
keen weather out of doors, so that he had
a good excuse for not venturing even so
far as the terraces.   He loitered out into
a large conservatory, and then found himself in the library—an immense room with
a gallery running round it, supported on
pillars of Derbyshire marble, and with black
oak shelves full of rare books, for the late

Lord St. Austell had been an inveterate and also a prudent collector. There was a small organ at one end, for the library occasionally did duty as a concert-room, and there were easy-chairs, and tables covered with the latest books from Mudie and Smith and Sons, and with the current reviews and magazines. No club library could have been better appointed or arranged.

Sir Hugo was not much given to reading, for which in his heart he had a certain contempt, believing that if a man knows anything which it is worth your while to know also, he will be much too careful over such a precious secret to put it in a book and make public property of it. But the glass doors of the library commanded the hall and the gallery which ran round it, so that as Lady St. Austell descended from the gallery by the grand staircase, it happened that Sir Hugo, having just laid down the *Builder*,—a weekly paper which he had seen at Boodles, but had never before interested himself in,—was emerging into the hall with the light firm step and upright bearing of an English gentleman who has done his duty before however painful it may have been, and is prepared to do it again at any sacrifice.

Lady St. Austell hoped Sir Hugo had breakfasted. Did he intend to go later in the day to the luncheon at the covert-side?

Sir Hugo was afraid that the day was rather cold. Lady St. Austell shared in that opinion. She doubted, indeed, if any of the ladies would go, except, perhaps, Lady Deepdale and her daughters, and some few others who seemed positively to revel in October air for its own sake. She herself was just about to visit the conservatories.

Now there is no conservatory attached to Boodles; and although Marcia had some favourite flowers of her own in a sort of glass sentry box over the portico in Sloane Street, Sir Hugo troubled himself as little about them as about many other things for which his daughter cared. He had heard of orchids, but did not like to hazard his reputation on the chance of their being in season. As to camelias he felt more certain, for he knew a camelia by sight, and had noticed some in the drawing-room the evening before, so he at once said that he should like to see the camelias, adding that a white camelia had always been his poor wife's favourite flower; and

then he shook his head as if he were looking back through the vista of past years,
and somehow seemed to find comfort in
the idea of camelias.

Now Lady St. Austell was proud of her
camelias, as Sir Hugo very well knew.
He had, in fact, noticed that the camelias
he had seen the evening before were freshly
cut, and had not come down by train
packed in wool. He consequently soon
found himself in the camelia house with
her ladyship, who although occupied in
tying little fragments of white ribbon to
the flowers she selected to be cut for the
evening, was yet not too engrossed in this
pursuit to compliment the exemplary father
on Marcia's appearance, and to add that
his daughter had a strong likeness to Sir
Hugo himself.

There was just enough truth in the compliment to have made it pleasant if you were perfectly certain of its sincerity; for people may tell the truth, and often do, without the least intention of doing so,— as when, to take a common instance, you are unwise enough to talk to a man whose name you do not know about a book whose author you have never met, and to express your opinion about that book with frankness, not being aware that you are talking to the man who wrote it.

Sir Hugo did a safe thing under all the circumstances. He sighed, and added that Marcia's health gave him great anxiety. Her ladyship hoped this apprehension was without foundation. At all events Marcia looked, if she might be allowed to say so, robust. Sir Hugo had his doubts. Might he, with the confidence of an old friend now in the sole charge of an only daughter, who was everything in life to him, take Lady St. Austell into his confidence. Certainly he might. So they went on selecting the camelias leisurely. Many of my readers must know from experience that there are pursuits which promote conversation. Angling is not one of these, but the choice of flowers is. So Sir Hugo began to talk.

"Marcia," said Sir Hugo, "is no longer a child, and she is lonely in my dungeon of a house in Sloane Street. I watch her carefully, and am sure that my eye is not deceived. She has, as far as my limited income permits, everything that she can wish. Her pets, her books, her flowers, and her little studio—for she has, I believe, so far as I can see, a genuine instinct for art. Of her music I can speak with confidence, and it is one of my greatest pleasures to take her to the opera. But I feel that I am no companion for her. Her governess, Fräulein Dietz, is a most accomplished and highly sympathetic lady. But I feel, dear Lady St. Austell, that it is hardly a wholesome life for a girl of Marcia's age to be living in that lonely house with her father, even although he is fortunately able to devote his time to her."

Lady St. Austell assented most cordially; but why did not Marcia go out into society?

"How can I take her out?" replied Sir Hugo. "I do what little I can, but my means are sadly straitened. You would be astonished," he added with a light laugh, "to see how simply we have to live. And I may also say how admirable a housekeeper Marcia makes. Without her our little *menage* could not possibly be carried on for a week. But there are not many years left me, and I must not allow her, even if I would, to sacrifice her young and bright life for me."

"Marcia ought to marry," said Lady St. Austell decidedly. "It is time she did so, and I do not see why she should not make a brilliant match."

Here was the ball at Sir Hugo's feet. It was the sole remaining object of his life, he declared, with perceptible emotion in his voice, to see his darling and only child comfortably settled, and if he might say so, in a position which he was certain she would adorn, and to the duties and responsibilities of which he knew she would prove equal.

"I can see no difficulty in the matter whatever," said her ladyship. "Marcia's appearance is striking. I may tell you that she has been talked about since your arrival. Even the old Duchess—and Heaven knows she doesn't often praise any one!—has been quite taken by her, and has been asking me all about her. I said of course that I knew Marcia's fortune was not large, but the Duchess laughed the idea of fortune out of the question, and said that Marcia could marry when she pleased, and wondered where the men had all been to allow her to remain single so long."

Sir Hugo again sighed. It was a sigh capable of many meanings. It expressed gratitude for Lady St. Austell's sympathy, deep affection for an only child, and an untold burden of anxiety as to the future and its possibilities. Sir Hugo managed that sigh and modulated it to perfection.

"There are men in the house at this moment," her ladyship cheerfully continued as she selected her flowers; "there is young Lord Norwich. He is not thirty, and he has seventy thousand a-year if a penny, as I need hardly tell you. It would be a splendid match for Marcia, and one that is quite within her reach. At least I can see no obstacle. Or there is Mr. Davidson, the iron-master, who I dare say could buy up three such men as Norwich if he wishes. He is a Radical in politics, as you know, and talks to you a great deal too much about his constituents, the puddlers of Coketown, who belong to him as much as does the place itself. But it is the fashion to be a radical in these days, and Mr. Davidson has many good points. He has raced his own yacht over the Atlantic and won by eleven hours. You must have read of that, and the men here are all agreed about him. I hear that he is a good shot, rides straight, and is as simple and unaffected as the school-boy that he still looks. I could name others,"—here a peculiarly choice camelia was selected,—"but these two are the pick of my party, cracks of my team, I think men call it when they are talking of horses. For myself," she added—here another was marked out for the gardener,— "I should give the preference to Davidson, who I am certain has a good deal in him,

and will modify his radical views as he
gets older, and feels the responsibilities
of his wealth." Another camelia was
selected.

Sir Hugo could hardly find words.
Might he rely on their old friendship?
Might he ask her to help him in this most
delicate, difficult, and responsible matter?
He felt it was one beyond his own powers,
needing a tact which he had never possessed, and which he had always felt was
an instinct, a natural gift, like Lady St.
Austell's own ear for music which he had
so often envied her.

Lady St. Austell laughed, and marked
another camelia. "There are no black
camelias," she said lightly, "any more,
my gardener tells me, than black roses.
Let us give Norwich the preference for

to-night, and the young king of coal and
iron can wait a day. Norwich shall take
your dear girl down to-night, and—well,
we will see."

CHAPTER VI.

LORD ST. AUSTELL looked, as many of our great landowners do, somewhat commonplace. Until he began to talk to you, or you noticed that easy charm of manner which I venture to tell Mr. Chamberlain is in England almost peculiar to the aristocracy, you would have taken him for a prosperous tenant farmer, or possibly even a squire of sufficient importance to be a justice of the peace. He was a cheerful, hearty, simple man, who having been born to his position and his wealth, took them as a matter of course. He was a good landlord; he was kind-hearted, and no man in the whole county was so popular among his own tenants and those of his neighbours.

English landowners of this type are becoming scarcer every year. They are survivals of Sir Roger de Coverley. Their kind seem doomed to extinction, and it is difficult to see who will take their place. Lord St. Austell was the wrong side of fifty, but as sturdy and hearty as ever, with just a grey hair here and there. He could walk thirty miles before dinner, take his wine afterwards, and sit chatting over his cigar and his one glass of whiskey and water while the younger men all round disappeared or fell asleep.

Her ladyship was some six or seven years his junior. She was a kind-hearted woman, but her kindness consisted in making up her mind somewhat at haphazard what was best for her favourites, and then insisting that it should be done. Lady St. Austell was most anxious to make you happy, but you must consent to be happy in her way and after her method, and not according to your own devices.

Edmund About has told us that the Roman Catholic Church holds it an article of faith that the Pope is infallible, and that the opinion is one to which the majority of Popes themselves become in time inclined. Lady St. Austell believed firmly in her own infallibility, and her husband encouraged the belief.

There was once an immense railway navvy who, when his comrades expostu-

lated with him *more suo* for allowing his
wife to beat him with the broom-stick,
replied philosophically that it amused her
and it didn't trouble him. In something
after this fashion Lady St. Austell was
allowed to rule; and although when she
approached a cottage the children were
sent up-stairs to hide under the bed, yet
the mothers knew that her ladyship was
at heart far more kindly than imperious,
and that she was always open to any tale
of distress, although, as it was observed,
you had to take your medicine as well
as your beef and flour and blankets, and
to swallow it too.

Nothing pleased her more than to have
her advice asked or her assistance called
in, as Sir Hugo very well knew; for her
character had hardly changed from what

it had been five-and-twenty years earlier, when there had been something like little love passages between the two during the London season, and when Sir Hugo still believed that he should make his mark in the world, and was especially calculated to shine in diplomacy. Her ladyship was still remarkably handsome—tall, erect, and with dark black hair and singularly expressive eyes. She might have been painted as Juno, or Margaret of Anjou, certainly not at any time of her life as an ideal of Tennyson's Enid.

Lord Pentreath, the only child of this happily assorted couple, was a young lieutenant, with as much military distinction as can be won in the Blues, and was at present shooting wolves in the Ardennes.

Having no daughters of her own, Lady

St. Austell liked to take a motherly interest in those of other people, and was always ready to lend herself to any scheme for their welfare, provided that she was properly approached in the first instance, with a due recognition of her judgment, tact, and other sterling qualities. And so she had, as she honestly believed, taken Marcia's welfare to heart as much as if she had been her own daughter; and here let me notice, as the reader may perhaps recollect, that there was a certain resemblance both of disposition and appearance between Lady St. Austell and Marcia which somehow attracted the elder woman to the younger, and made it a pleasure, as well as a self-imposed duty, to promote her ultimate happiness in life.

All people with warm hearts are liable

to errors of judgment, in which they sometimes obstinately persist; but on the whole
they do more good in the world than
harm, as it is better for the bulk of young
people that they should shape their own
course of life as little as possible. Only
Marcia was not like the bulk of young
ladies, and was quite able to make up her
mind for herself, though quite amenable
to persuasion when her feelings of affection
were in any way roused.

Marcia's day—for I must return to her
at last—had passed pleasantly enough.
There had been a sort of excursion in three
or four roomy breaks, with an attendant
flotilla of pony carriages, to some ruins in
the neighbourhood, which were, like all
other old ruins, very interesting to those
who could reconstruct them in imagination,

and utterly devoid of interest to those who looked at ruins as things to be sketched or photographed, or painted for the Academy, and not as the fossil homes of history.

I remember being one of the party that drove over from Carmarthen to Llanstephan, and I can declare that the only one who appreciated the ruins thoroughly, and explored every part of it, was an American who had lived all his life in the Southern States, and who showed his wisdom by saying as little as possible.

There was five o'clock tea, of course, and dinner this evening was at seven, as usual. When every one was in the drawing-room, and awaiting the welcome sound of the gong, Lady St. Austell entrusted Marcia to Lord Norwich. That young gentleman was a mild, pleasant man of the Saxon type, with light curly hair and blue eyes. He had not much to say, nor was what little he had to say about anything in particular, nor, if it had been, would it probably have been profound; but at any rate it was to the point. And he was intensely good-natured, and still as vivacious as when his exuberant spirits used to lead to his being "sent up" at Eton with unpleasant frequency. He had been in the Grenadiers for three or four years, and had left soon after his father died. For he was shrewd enough to know that the owner's eye makes the acre rise in value. But he had still about him all that one really likes in an English schoolboy. He enjoyed any and every form of sport, from shooting a grizzly bear down—I am sorry to say—to drawing that terrible animal's little British cousin, the badger. Perhaps I can best describe him by saying, that if he were laughed at over a fall in the hunting-field, or if his neighbour wiped his eye among the stubbles, he neither showed temper at the time nor bore malice afterwards.

Lord Norwich was kind to his dependants, not with any ultimate object, but because it really pleased him to make people happy; and I am afraid that this really pleasant side in his character led to his being sadly victimized,—as, for instance, by the architect who designed his model cottages, and the builder who condescended to superintend their construction.

"And how do you like St. Austell,

Miss Conyers?" Lord Norwich commenced by way of safety.

Marcia had never seen such a place before. She was charmed with it. Now Lord Norwich knew half the county houses in England, but instead of saying so, and treating her to long descriptions of places she had never seen, he chatted about St. Austell itself, and thence got to the ruins Marcia had visited that afternoon.

This led then somehow to the cities of Bashan, of which she had read and which Lord Norwich had seen. And then they got to a relic of Upper Syria on his watch-chain—the claw of a Syrian bear he had shot in Lebanon; and at last Marcia found herself talking as fluently as if she were sitting in the twilight over the fire with Fräulein Dietz. It was a novelty to sit

by a man who could talk vivaciously and
yet without even the suspicion of egotism
about places which it was one of the
secret wishes of Marcia's heart to see ; and
when Lord Norwich gave her an idea of
the Sea of Galilee as he first saw it when
he left his tent in the morning, having
camped after dark, Marcia so lost herself
in interest that she hardly noticed what
was going on. And this of course was
wrong, for conversation at dinner ought to
be general, wherefore it was said by Brillat
Savarin, that the number at table should
never exceed that of the Muses or fall
below that of the Graces, on the ground
that good conversation and pleasant is the
best possible promoter of sound digestion,
and that if you get beyond nine you split
up into knots, making not one dinner, but

two or three; whereas, if there are only two of you, it is certain that the one will bore the other.

But with our big dinner-parties you must accept your fate, and make the most of your next door neighbours.

Nearly opposite to Marcia sat John Douglas, who was doing his best to extract something better than monosyllables from Miss Heythrop, whose conversational powers were extremely limited.

Miss Heythrop was the daughter of a fox-hunting baronet, of whom it was said at his club by a good-natured friend, that it was unfair to call Heythrop stupid, and to declare that he had not two ideas in his head. On the contrary, that receptacle always contained exactly a couple, for when once a third made its way into it, it played the young cuckoo in the nest, and was sure to eject one of the others.

Miss Heythrop had somewhat more imagination than her father, and hardly did herself justice. You were apt to think her more stupid than she really was. But her stupidity, much of which was due to an unfortunate shyness, ceased to irritate when you came across what a Californian would term the genuine streak of good nature and freshness which is so common in English girls who have been brought up at home.

John Douglas had time to look across the table, and somehow or another he did not like what he saw, for he had begun to become interested in Marcia, and he entertained but a poor opinion of Lord Norwich, whom he regarded as an empty-

I

headed young fellow. And herein he was doubly wrong. In the first place, you have no business to regard a young lady whom you may happen to admire as being more or less your exclusive property; and secondly, however clever you may be yourself, you are never safe in putting a man down for a fool until you have known him for a very considerable time. These are rules of life which can only become branded into you by that awkward and unpleasant kind of experience which follows upon frequent defeats, occasionally at the hands of men whom you have some right to consider inferior to yourself. I do not say that Lord Norwich was not a most estimable young nobleman, of average intelligence and unblemished character. I may add that Douglas knew as much—except, perhaps, that he underrated the intelligence. But it irritated him to see Lord Norwich sitting by Marcia and engrossing her. Men of high ability who have deliberately preferred active life to the life of the library, are yet in their way as petulant as a scholar whose latinity is called in question. And John Douglas was not yet superior to this kind of vanity. Men indeed are far more vain than women. It is in their nature, as in that of birds, to ruffle their plumes, and strut, and show themselves.

If you want a canary to sing you must give him another canary to sing against, or you must hang up a looking-glass, in which he sees a rival with distended chest and undulating throat. The old story that the nightingale is a good husband singing to his beloved mate is a fiction only equal to that which represents the robin redbreast as a tender-hearted creature, living upon bread crumbs.

"Come out!" cries the cock nightingale to a rival whom he hears in the distance. "Come out! Come out here! Here! Here! Come here! Come out! Come here!" This is his exquisite trill.

And this fierce instinct still remains latent in man. The slightest circumstance will bring it to the surface in a moment. Douglas, as he sat at table, was literally fidgetting for a pretext to quarrel with poor Lord Norwich; and if he could have bitten his thumb at him he would probably have done so immediately the ladies had left.

CHAPTER VII.

NEXT day the coverts had a rest, and there was nothing to be done except to kill time. Lord Norwich, who had won the hearts of the gamekeepers, repaired, with one or two other choice spirits who knew of the secret, to the home farm, where the select company spent some hours in worrying a badger, who having been only two days caught, was aggressive and vindictive in his manner, and by no means disposed to recognize a fox-terrier two-thirds his own weight as an acquaintance with whom to familiarize.

Many people consider badger-baiting a
brutal sport. So it is if the dog be three
or four times the size of the badger, or the
badger twice the weight of the dog. I
myself, at a certain canine repository not a
mile from Charing Cross, have seen a
badger with one grip of his jaws tear off
the leg of a dog at the shoulder. And a
very sickening sight it was! All field
sports are brutal more or less, and the
excuse for badger-baiting is identical with
that for cub-hunting—it is part of a dog's
education, and as such is sometimes said to
deserve the recognition of country gentlemen. It certainly is not more cruel than
otter-hunting, in which, especially if the
spear be not allowed, many of the hounds
are always terribly wounded, while the fate
of the otter, if he be not promptly tailed

for the sake of his skin, is not a picture for humanitarians to consider.

Others of the company repaired to the fir-wood in quest of cock. Most sportsmen will agree with me that there is no sport so keen as that of bringing down a wood-cock ; and it is certainly a fact that Chantrey, who once killed three cock at a shot, devoted some weeks to commemorating the feat in a marble bas-relief.

"Driven from northern climes that would have starved them,
    Chantrey first shot and then he carved them."

John Douglas was somehow missing. He said something at breakfast about a sort of sprain in his ankle. Anyhow he did not go badger-baiting or cock-shooting, but took a little more than usual care over his morning apparel, and hung about the house and its precincts.

It is one of the great pleasures of stopping in a large country house at the same time with other guests, that you can stray about and do as you please without being considered to violate the proprieties, or even to be guilty of eccentricity. In fact, you are more or less asked for the express purpose of doing as you please, unless your services should be specially required.

You may hunt out the stables, armed with a clay pipe, look at the horses, talk to the grooms, and defer to the superior knowledge of the pad groom and the coachman. Or you may send a request to the head gardener to show you over his hot-houses and forcing-pits. This you will find an expensive tour, gardeners being less sociable than grooms, and more alive to the sight of a half sovereign.

Or you can stroll round to the houses of the keepers, where you are sure to find enough to interest you if you care in the least either for sport in its ordinary acceptation, or for natural history as Gilbert White understood it. The keeper's lodge indeed is, if he be equal to his work and responsibilities, a small museum of the natural history of the county. I will leave the home farm out of the question. No man cares for cows or pigs or poultry unless he owns land of his own.

Instead of visiting hot-houses, or the keeper's lodge, or the home farm, Douglas sauntered about the house—a place so huge that your movements attracted but little attention. First, by way of keeping up appearances, he strolled into the billiard-room, which he found deserted, with the brown holland over the table, and the heavy iron preparing itself for work over a little brazier of glowing charcoal. The library was also vacant. It is a curious fact that leather-binding — especially morocco leather—seems to gather strength in the night and to smell more powerfully in the morning, as we are told that flowers do when the dew is upon them. Perhaps John Douglas may have disliked the smell of morocco, or may not have felt disposed to glance over Audubon's *Birds of America*, in elephant folio. Anyhow, he passed through the side door of the library into what was known as the writing-room, because it had one or two small tables in it at which you could write if you pleased, and a letter-box on the mantelpiece, letters dropped into which fell through the wall into a miniature pillar-box in the hall. And here, oddly enough, were Marcia and the Duchess of Lincoln. The Duchess was welcome to him. Her presence gave him time to collect himself, or, as sporting gentlemen say, pull himself together.

Besides, she was, as the phrase goes, a dear, good, kind old lady, who was never in the way, and might in fact, with infinite advantage to her young friends, have put herself in the way more often than she did.

The duchess kindly commenced the conversation. She thought it was a fine day. Douglas agreed. He was sorry to be a prisoner, but was detained in the house sorely against his will by a sprained ankle. The duchess had heard that a sprained ankle should be rubbed with a judicious mixture of yellow soap, brown sugar, spirits of hartshorn, and Scotch whiskey, and should then be sewn up in unbleached flannel and allowed entire rest. Douglas promised to try this famous cure if he were not better within a few hours. Marcia, appealed to by her Grace, had no experience in the treatment of sprained ankles, but had been told by Fräulein Dietz that bruised poppy heads—the big poppy heads that you see in big jars in the windows of chemist's shops—were a sovereign specific in the shape of a poultice, and alleviated pain almost magically.

The Duchess considered poppy-heads dangerous. You might take too much of them, as you might chlorodyne. She had heard, moreover, that laudanum was made

from poppies, and had never herself coun-
tenanced the practise of rubbing it into the
face for toothache.

Douglas had to explain that his accident
was slight, and probably only needed rest.
He would be all right in four-and-twenty
hours. Meantime, in such glorious air, and
in a house with chambers of such proportions, one could well forego violent exercise
for so short a period. Then the conversation became general, and in its course
Douglas succeeded fully in securing something more than the Duchess's transient
good opinion. She knew that he was a
barrister, and had expected to find him
something after the type of the majority
of barristers described in fiction—a sort of
Mr. Serjeant Striver.

Clearly this young man could not belong

to this class, and as the Duchess had just formulated this opinion, she was summoned by her maid, who came to say that his Grace would like to see her for a few minutes.   And so it came to pass that Douglas and Marcia were left alone.

What was the conversation about, and how was it carried on?   I cannot tell you, for the simple reason that it was natural, and so wandered from one subject to another.   They talked about field sports, and Scotch scenery, and Highland customs, and yachting, and then of even lighter things, such as the last opera, and the last novel, and the latest variety of chrysanthemums, and a book of travel that had just set all London talking, because a number of people who knew all about it declared it to be a tissue of inventions, and were in their turn denounced by a number of other people who knew all about it as being animated by personal jealousy. It had been the "gorilla book" of the season, and they had both read it.

Now I do not believe in love at first sight. But it is quite possible upon a very short acquaintance for a feeling to spring into existence which may easily develop, according to the circumstances, into either love or strong friendship. Marcia, to use an old expression which, like many of its kind, is extremely felicitous, was "taken" (not the French *épris*, but our honest English taken) with this young man, whom she knew to be so clever, and who yet was so simple and almost youthful in his manner, and who took so pleasant and keen an interest in simple things. Douglas, on the other hand, found in Marcia a something unlike what you would expect to find in a young lady of her age, inasmuch as she was grave and thoughtful and intelligent; and as his mind reverted to the Duchess, who had so opportunely left them, it occurred to him that in the fitness of things Marcia was suited to be a Duchess, if not indeed obviously intended for that exalted position. And this was a dangerous frame of mind, both for Marcia on her part and for Douglas on his own. And as I do not intend to take down my Shakespeare to remind myself how Othello and Desdemona fell in love, I will not pursue the parallel, although in many points it would be similar, or to say the least, suggestive. For Sir Hugo had many points in him which resembled Brabantio,

although he lacked much of that old gentleman's dignity.

How the conversation might have ended
or into what channels it might have strayed
I am not prepared to state, but it was
interrupted by the appearance on the scene
of Lady Gwendoline Anstice, who burst into
the room like a tornado, in quest, or pretended quest, of a novel which she thought
she must have left there, plunged at once
into the conversation, and began to flounder
about in it after her own most helpless
fashion, and evinced not the least intention
of taking her departure.

Lady Gwendoline talked in much the
same monotonous fashion as that in which
a water-spout with a leak in it will drip
in rainy weather, and I believe was under
the honest delusion that she had excep-

tional conversational gifts. Marcia did not like to go, and Douglas on his part saw that to take his departure would be a false move. So they sat still, and Lady Gwendoline cackled to them.

I dislike slang, but can conscientiously declare that cackle is the only word in the English language which expresses my meaning.

And here let me give a word of advice to ladies who, finding themselves, let us kindly say, nearer thirty-two or even thirty-five than they care to generally admit, and who, having read of Madame de Stael and other such ornaments of French *salons*, endeavour to cultivate the art of conversation —perhaps the most difficult of all arts, and one in which the very greatest men have often conspicuously failed. A young lady should not talk as if she felt it incumbent upon her to join in the conversation; on the contrary, she should rather endeavour to say just enough to show that she is following it and is interested by it. She is usually troublesome if she endeavours to take a leading part, and still more troublesome if she asks frivolous questions.

Now Lady Gwendoline would without hesitation have plunged into the lunar theory with an Astronomer Royal, or have taken Mr. Browning to task over his *Paracelsus.* She talked for the sake of talking, and her conversation was consequently as vacant and wearying as the whistle of a railway porter when he has nothing to do but to loiter about the platform with his hands in his pockets.

On the other hand, Lady Gwendoline

Anstice knew very well how to manage a
stupid man, and if she found herself out
of her depth with John Douglas, could
have succeeded to a marvel with Lord
Norwich.

And if the truth must be told, Lady
Gwendoline had set her cap at Lord
Norwich, and ably assisted by her mother,
Lady Deepdale (a match-maker of wide
experience and acknowledged success), was
at present engaged in laying siege to that
eligible young nobleman.

This made her, of course, anxious to
annoy Marcia, who, she took it for granted,
had, as she would have phrased it herself,
intended business with Lord Norwich last
night, and was only keeping in her hand
with this young barrister in the morning.
So she remained out of mere spite, or as

ladies, I believe, term it, "aggravation,"
—the corresponding Americanese is, as
I understand, "cussedness,"—pouring out
a ceaseless flood of nothings until the
luncheon-bell rang.

The party at lunch included Sir Hugo,
of course, Douglas, and nearly all the ladies,
from her Grace downwards, although most
of the men were absent. Lord Norwich
came in from his morning's sport with a
strong aroma about him of tobacco-smoke
and the stable, not unmixed with a stronger
flavour, in which an experienced nose would
at once have detected the peculiar fragrance
of a badger, an animal ranking in this
particular gift of nature next only to the
polecat.

An awkward attempt to mask his morning pursuits with eau de cologne had only

intensified the evidence against him and aggravated the offence. He made himself, however, entertaining after his own fashion to Marcia, so that her father was greatly pleased, and began to consider that his self-sacrifice in leaving Boodles would, like other virtuous actions, have its own reward, —a portion of which he anticipated in the shape of some peculiarly choice Madeira, thoughtfully tendered him by the head butler.

Lunch ended as lunch ought to, it being a meal which is somehow understood to be like breakfast, with no definite beginning or end, and consequently not requiring the solemnity of initial or final invocation or thanksgiving, even although a bishop may be present in the full glory of his gaiters and upright collar. The guests straggled out as they had straggled in, and Marcia soon found herself dressed for a cold day, and waiting under the colonnade for Lady St. Austell, with whom she was to drive down to the bridge, and so across the river, and back through the woods. She had barely time to admire the indications given by the long colonnade of its summer glories, before the victoria arrived, and Marcia found herself side by side with her kindly hostess, covered with a rug of priceless silver fox, and rattling briskly down the avenue, glorious even in winter, past the home farm and the kangaroo sheds, over the lake, past the rookery and the deer, and so at last in the open road.

And here it was, when the rattle of the feet of the stout little cobs rendered the conversation inaudible to the solemn and

self-absorbed occupants of the box, that
Lady St. Austell took up her parable.

I will not undertake to describe her
ladyship's manner or method.   Each in
its way was perfect.   She was kindness
itself to Marcia, speaking to her in the
manner of a mother, which she was able
to assume at once, by explaining that the
rug which Marcia so much admired consisted of skins perhaps the most prized in
the world, because the rarest, with the
exception of sable and ermine.   They were
trophies of the chase, brought home by her
son from the extreme north of Canada,—
in fact, out the Hudson's Bay territory; and
so from eulogy of her son's skill and power
of endurance as a Nimrod, she glided into
discreet praise of young Norwich, whose
many manly virtues she extolled with the

utmost tact. She had heard that he rode magnificently to hounds, and had ridden second on his own horse for the Grand Military at Sandown, securing it the next year on a chestnut, the property of his Colonel, and so vicious as to be a terror to the oldest rough-riders at Knightsbridge and Windsor.

This led her to descant not only upon Lord Norwich's excellent qualities, but also upon his position, with its wealth and its responsibilities—wealth almost beyond the power of man to exhaust, and possibilities that would be infinite if only his undoubted natural abilities were stimulated and directed into the proper channel by sympathy and tact. This eulogy, though most adroitly planned and phrased, somehow hung fire with Marcia, who could

not help thinking for the life of her of
the immense difference, when all was said,
that separated Lord Norwich, with all his
good nature and versatility, from the re-
served and masterful John Douglas.   It
was the difference almost between Prince
Rupert and John Hampden—each of whom
was beyond question the highest ornament of the side on which he drew his
sword.

I wish to say nothing unkind of Lord
Norwich.   I will prove as much by de-
claring my conviction that he was brave,
generous, and utterly incapable of anything
unworthy either in act or thought, differing
herein from many other young men of his
age and liable to his temptations.   But in
her own mind Marcia never even dreamed
of comparing him with Douglas.   Indeed,

the two men were so utterly dissimilar in every way that the only comparison was one which intensified the contrast.

So that when Lady St. Austell began to somehow suggest that Lord Norwich, with his title, his wealth, his infinite good-nature, and his many sterling qualities, would make an excellent husband, and deserved a wife who would appreciate him and stimulate him to something higher and more worthy of his abilities than the chase and the race-course, Marcia hardly, if at all, caught the drift of her ladyship's praise of this young man ; and while agreeing with all that fell from her hostess of well-deserved encomium, failed to see how it in any way concerned herself, until Lady St. Austell, in the most simple manner possible —and truth to tell, with almost Bismarkian bluntness—came straight to the point by expressing her conviction, in fact, she might say her knowledge, that Lord Norwich admired Marcia greatly, and that he would be, apart altogether from his position, a husband of whom any girl might be proud.

This fairly startled Marcia out of all her usual self-possession, and she found herself almost stammering out that she was fully alive to these excellent qualities which Lord Norwich undoubtedly possessed, and which lay evidently and unmistakably upon the surface, but that the idea of becoming Lady Norwich had never crossed her mind, and took her entirely by surprise. Wherein she was speaking the exact truth, as young ladies usually do when an intelligible proposition is laid before them which requires an immediate answer, and, if I may say so, takes them unawares.

Marcia could only murmur something in general praise of the object of discussion which she did with obvious sincerity. For his frankness and good-nature were beyond all question genuine, and Marcia felt honestly that her ladyship had gone little, if at all, in her praise further than the limits of exact truth. So she could only say that it was impossible to meet Lord Norwich without seeing at once his many admirable qualities, and above all his utter absence of anything like egotism, his evident kindness of heart, and his extreme good-nature.

And as Marcia put all this in her own way, instead of in the phraseology I have chosen to summarize it, Lady St. Austell had the penetration to see that she was saying exactly what she meant, and had also the tact to divert the conversation into other channels, and for the present to wait upon events instead of precipitating them.

CHAPTER VIII.

THAT evening there was a dinner-party at St. Austell Towers. There was the lord-lieutenant, with his wife and two daughters; and there was the Bishop of the diocese, also accompanied by his wife, three eligible daughters, and his domestic chaplain.

The lord-lieutenant was a tall, largely built man, with no power of consecutive thought, and certainly none of consecutive conversation. He detested railroads, which he believed had lowered prices all over the country, and made the working classes far too independent. His general appearance was that of a sergeant-major in a regiment of heavy dragoons. He stood with his legs wide apart, talked in the tone of voice of an adjutant in the orderly room, and occasionally indulged in an oath. He did not approve of swearing in the abstract, but he considered it a duty to use a little strong language about such things as Mr. Gladstone's latest speech, and the turnip fly, and the increase of poaching, thereby asserting his position, and showing that he was not one of the ordinary herd, who under an Act of Parliament still in force can be, and sometimes are, fined five shillings for each profane word they use. He was very pompous, very prejudiced, very stupid, and very kind-hearted.

The Bishop might have been taken for

a butler had it not been for his buckles, apron, purple coat with turned-up collar, and other outward and visible signs of the inward and episcopal grace. He had been seventh wrangler. He had edited the Epistle to the Galatians, and he had a large family of daughters whom he planted out in marriage year after year, providing for his sons-in-law out of the livings in his gift. In reality he was a shrewd man of the world, and would have given much to have been able to begin life over again.

There was of course the usual allowance of county squires and gentlemen, and there was Lord St. Austell's agent, a fat man with a fat watch-chain, who kept himself in a corner as if he were present on suffrance. And most of these guests had brought their wives, and some their sons and daughters, so that the immense room would have appeared full were it not that lord-lieutenants and bishops and other peers of the realm dwarf ordinary folk, until you are hardly aware of their presence or even existence.

Let me give the conversation for once and for all. It was the ordinary conversation at St. Austell Towers. You can hear it at all large country houses. Much of it wearied Marcia, not a little of it made her almost indignant.

A neighbouring squire declared that it was impossible to make sheep pay. The importation of all foreign cattle ought to be stopped, and he would not even mind a heavy duty on tinned meat, which lowered the price of home produce, and was usually very unwholesome.

Lord St Austell was very doubtful whether farming would pay its way for many years longer. No doubt steam had been a great blessing in many ways. But in others it had been of doubtful advantage; and he wanted to know what the farmers were to do when all our great towns got their butter and eggs from France and their cheese from Normandy, and when corn from the Danube was so cheap that it no longer paid a tenant farmer to grow sound red wheat?

A colonel of hussars from York opined that it was the radicals who did all the mischief,—men like Cobden, and Bright, and Chamberlain who set class against class.

The Bishop considered that to set class against class was sinful. The earth was the Lord's and the fulness thereof; and it was not for man to repine when Providence showered its bounties on him. And he then finished the half breast of a particularly fine woodcock.

The Bishop's chaplain was stimulated by this into the expression of his conviction that the poor were being educated above their station, and that discontent was the inevitable consequence.

Lady St Austell could confirm the fact. It was almost impossible to get a good domestic servant, and as soon as you had secured one, and she had learnt her duties, and saved twenty pounds, she was sure to marry some worthless fellow from the nearest town, and emigrate with him. It was really dreadful, and it would soon become a very serious question what we were to do for servants at all.

So the conversation rambled on, and Marcia found it intolerably dull and even irritating. But there is an end to everything, even to a dinner of ceremony, and it was a relief to follow in the train of Lady St. Austell to the drawing-room, where the ladies, until the men joined them, talked about nothing at all, infusing into that substratum just enough of venom to make it piquant.

Before long the men arrived upon the scene, and to Marcia's pleasure John Douglas somehow singled her out at once, and came up with still a marked lameness, but otherwise looking—I speak for men— as fine and well-built a young giant as any one in the room.

Sir Hugo had been drinking Chambertin. This most excellent of parents could carry his liquor with any man. But, on the other hand, Chambertin is a wine which has peculiar virtues of its own. It has a delicious bouquet, and it is very strong. It is a wine that young men do not appreciate as they ought, and which their seniors are sometimes apt to appreciate rather more than is good for them.

Sir Hugo seemed to feel his veins expanding, and began again to think of how comfortably he could live in lodgings somewhere near his Club if he could only get the house in Sloane Street off his hands. He consequently looked round about with the purest of paternal motives to see what Marcia was doing, and how she was improving the shining hour. He noticed that she was talking to Douglas and not either Lord Norwich or Mr. Davidson. But the

Chambertin made him disposed to take all things cheerfully, and a cup of coffee so steadied his nerves that a little later in the evening, when the ladies had finally departed, he took a hand at whist, and in the end went to bed with his heart full of the most noble sentiments, and his waistcoat pocket of half-sovereigns.

Douglas mean time was talking earnestly to Marcia, and, as it were, cross-examining her. There was much in her that was certain to please a man of his temperament. We all know what Byron says of a certain large class of young ladies—

"The nursery still lisps out in all they utter;
    Besides, they always smell of bread and butter."

Marcia had nothing about her of the school in question. And so the two were soon busily engaged.

Good Burgundy makes a man bold if he has been wise enough to take it in moderation. The presence of a handsome woman puts him upon his metal. Other causes may easily concur to make him more or less self-confident, possibly with sufficient reason. I know a man who said, and I believe truthfully, that he had never "proposed," as the term is, but once in his life, and that even then he was not aware that he had done so until the fact was brought home to him the next morning. And he found himself married before a month was over without having the faintest notion how it all came about.

John Douglas was hardly of this type. I am not going to give my readers exactly what he said, but it was simple and to the point. It ended by his telling Marcia that he should find out Sir Hugo immediately after lunch the next day, and by his begging a camelia pinned in her dress to nerve him for the encounter.

It is curious that when a man is in earnest his jokes, unless bitter, are sure to be intensely feeble, and his attention to really unimportant trifles excessive. But we are all the creatures of convention. "Mr. Sambo," says the gentleman with the bones to the gentleman with the banjo, "you say something funny." Why this should be the invariable prelude to a negro melody I have always failed to understand. So I have never been able to see why, from time almost immemorial down to the day when Corisande gave Lothair a rose, the gift of a flower should be a thing almost as full of consequences as was once the plucking of an apple. I do not attempt to explain the fact; I only state it. And I may add, that the flower imparted some sort of indefinite charm to John Douglas' disposition and manner. For whereas earlier in the day he had irreverently spoken of Sir Hugo to one or two of the other men as being an old ass, he now seemed disposed to extend to him a certain measure of toleration, if not indeed of positive respect; and whereas he had also somewhat snubbed poor harmless, good-natured Lord Norwich, he now condescended to chat with him pleasantly about things in general, even down to the chances for next year's Derby and the latest innovations in burlesque. So that his lordship next day spoke of Douglas to the other men as being a devilish clever fellow, and not at all stuck-up. And this will show my readers how easy it is to make yourself pleasant if you will only take the very slightest amount of trouble.

As for Marcia, I need not set out at length what was passing through her mind. But I shall do no harm if I give a few salient points. She had a contempt for her father which she had never consciously avowed to herself until it dawned upon her that she could change the whole tenor of her existence, and leave him actually the more comfortable for the change.

He would have his club and a bed-room in St. James' Street, or somewhere close off it. He might even take a set of chambers and keep a man-servant at a less expense than that entailed by the melancholy old house in Sloane Street. He

would be more comfortable and more at
his ease in every way, and Marcia felt
sure that her father would bear the shock
with fortitude of the most approved stage
stamp.

All this flashed upon her at once. Then,
too, she would also be able to provide a
comfortable home for dear old Fräulein
Dietz—a home where she would have no
little worries and anxieties, and would be
able, as it were, to sun herself and to
enjoy the luxury of doing nothing with no
responsibility attached to the doing of it.
And besides, she had made up her mind
that she liked John Douglas, and although
his proposal had come upon her most
unexpectedly she never hesitated for a
moment in accepting it. She could see
that he was a man who meant to make

his mark, and she felt certain that she could help him. And she liked him better than any one she had ever known. Beyond this she did not extend her horizon.

She did not calculate on the possibilities open to Douglas, of the ermine, or possibly of the woolsack. She was quite content, and more than content, to share his fortunes as they were. Other things occurred to her upon which I need not dwell, but which in no way altered her resolution, serving rather, indeed, to fortify it. And the board being thus cleared, she, both in metaphor and physically, put down her foot and resolved that she would marry John Douglas at any cost, checking herself, like a fair-minded girl as she was, by the reflection that there was no cost in the matter to anybody concerned, unless indeed it were to Douglas himself, who might perhaps have waited a little longer and done a great deal better. Even this she hardly admitted in her own heart, and so it did not much discomfort her.

Lord Norwich she thought of almost tenderly, but prudently concluded that he would soon find consolation elsewhere, even if he liked her as much as Lady St. Austell had declared. And so ended her reflections.

Lord Norwich, on his own part, was smoking a big cigar before his bedroom fire, and moistening it with whiskey and soda. I make no imputation of intemperance, for the whiskey was largely diluted, and an Eton boy might have drunk a pint of the mixture with impunity.

And so one by one the lights in the great house, not unlike human lives, were

either extinguished or allowed to burn
down in their sockets; and nothing broke
the silence except the clock from the tower,
with perhaps now and again the yelp or
bay of a hound from the kennels.

CHAPTER IX.

EARLY next morning John Douglas breakfasted with such of the party that were assembled, and waited patiently for Sir Hugo. He ascertained that coffee and other light refreshments, together with the *Morning Post* and his letters, had been sent up to that gentleman's room. So Douglas sauntered about the house, first taking due precaution that he should be at once informed of Sir Hugo's descent. He would have enjoyed a cigar on the terrace, but he knew that the smell of tobacco about him might possibly give Sir

Hugo a handle for an objection to his habits and general mode of life. So he resorted to the billiard room, where he amused himself by what is called knocking about the balls. This is an occupation which seems to comfort men pretty much as knitting comforts women. It gives them something to do, and so relieves the irritation always produced in an active mind by absolute physical idleness.

On the other hand, you can practise the most complicated cannons, and the boldest of winning, together with the subtlest of losing hazards, and be thinking of something else the whole time. The charm of all this is broken at once if you play yourself plain against spot, or spot against plain, which makes you lose your temper with yourself, and viciously concentrate your attention on the science of kinetics, thereby upsetting the philosophic equilibrium of your mind.

Douglas was in the midst of what for a mere amateur was a really fair run of spot strokes, when he was informed by an attendant, who had had what barristers' clerks call a special retainer, that Sir Hugo had descended, and was in fact occupied in the breakfast room. Repairing thither, Douglas found the occupation in question to consist in artistic appreciation of a Perigord pie and a glass of chablis— excellent things, which may be safely recommended by the youngest of physicians to the most anxious of parents whose system required support, or, for the matter of that, to anybody whose taste is sufficiently cultured to appreciate flavours so delicate as those of the truffle, and a wine which after all differs little, except as a matter of curiosity, from Chateau Yquem.

Douglas, by way of excuse for entering the room, broke a biscuit and just tasted a small cup of coffee. Sir Hugo, always good-natured when he had no immediate troubles or wants, and nothing to remotely rouse his selfishness into action or even suspicion, opined jocularly that Douglas had been sitting up late. Douglas replied that he had been up for some hours, and had really been waiting to see Sir Hugo. Sir Hugo allowed himself a stare which did not exceed the bounds of civility, and wondered to himself what the devil was coming.

These were his exact words, as he afterwards told the story to one of his most intimate friends at Boodles.

Then began an encounter in which there was really some brilliant fence; and as the servants began to appear upon the scene, an adjournment by tacit consent was made to the terrace. Douglas began by informing Sir Hugo of his position and prospects. This a fencing master would call an engagement in prime. Sir Hugo, guessing what was coming, parried it at once. He congratulated Douglas heartily. It was always pleasant, he observed with a sigh, to old fellows like himself who were going down the hill to see a young man making way up it, and to know that he was putting his best years to better purpose than they themselves had done. At the same time, nothing in life was certain. Even land, he added, in these Radical days seem to melt in your fingers.

Douglas agreed that land had been much affected of late years by legislation of an advanced Liberal character, but added that there were other investments, such as the funds, which were absolutely safe, and differed from land as involving less trouble in their management. He wished, however, he continued, to speak to Sir Hugo about an entirely different matter. He wished, in fact, to ask Sir Hugo's sanction to a promise Miss Conyers had already given him.

Sir Hugo in the most gentlemanly way exclaimed, "God bless my soul!" Mr. Hare himself could not have given the four words more of an old gentleman's dignity and sense of responsibility, and Douglas found himself once again disengaged.

"I had the permission of Miss Conyers herself," he exclaimed, "to speak to you

as I have, and I shall be glad—in fact,
it will be a duty—to inform you in
what quarters you can obtain independent
information as to my present position,
and what I think are my reasonable
prospects in life."

Nothing would have gratified Sir Hugo
more had time permitted it. He had, in
fact, heard himself of the rising reputation
of Mr. Douglas, and of many other things
that spoke highly—he might say most
highly—in his favour. But the welfare of
his only daughter—he ought rather to have
said his only child—had been, since her
lamented mother's death, the one thing
that bound him to this world. When he
had once seen her settled as he wished,
he should feel that his own work in life
was concluded and his labours over. And

—here he succeeded in the adroit manœuvre of disengagement immediately under the wrist—he might tell Mr. Douglas in confidence, and as a man of the world and also a man of honour speaking to another, that his daughter's marriage was a thing almost settled. "And so," he added, extending his hand frankly to Douglas, "let us, my dear sir, regard this conversation as if it had never taken place, and hope that it may end matters which when fully and frankly explained, as I hope I have endeavoured to do, need cause no trouble and give rise to no regret."

All this was very pretty, but I may add that it was altogether too much for Douglas. You can argue with the most dogmatic judge on the Bench, because he cannot dismiss you with platitudes. But there is no arguing with a man who firmly and politely declines to argue at all, and Douglas very nearly lost his temper.

"I have told you, Sir Hugo," he said, "that I have already the consent of Miss Conyers herself. Until she recalls that consent as explicitly as she has given it to me, I can only regret your refusal to sanction it. More than this I need hardly say, except that you must not consider me for a moment to regard your own decision just announced to me as in any way ending the matter."

Sir Hugo assented as courteously as if they had been discussing the most ordinary matter, requiring nothing but grace and tact and polish for its successful management. He made a slight gesture indicating, in a manner worthy of the great monarch himself, that it was in his power when he chose to bow with consummate grace, but that for the present, at any rate, his bow was a courtesy of civilized warfare and nothing more.

Douglas, on his part, answered with a stiff inclination of the body capable of many interpretations, all more or less uncomplimentary, and so turned upon his heel. It is astonishing how much can be compressed into a bow if you have that much passing through your mind at the time, and intend to distinctly let as much be understood.

And so the two men parted, Douglas after all not much disconcerted, and Sir Hugo, in spite of his imperturbable manner, in reality full of wrath, as most men are who have lived to secure their own selfish

purposes, and have somehow not exactly succeeded. For he could see that John Douglas
had sufficient force of character to prove
very troublesome, and certainly did not need
to be told that Marcia, in all matters of
real importance, had a will of her own.

So in a vague kind of way he foresaw
trouble,—that is to say, personal annoyance and discomfort. And he even began
to wonder seriously whether it would not
be best to make some inquiries, and perhaps
to give his consent upon conditions which
would rid him of the gloomy house in
Sloane Street, and enable him to spend
the remainder of his days in well-earned
comfort. After all, he reflected, with a
complacency worthy of Mr. Turveydrop
himself, there was no certainty that Marcia
would marry either Lord Norwich or the

ironmaster, or, for the matter of that, that either of them would offer himself as a son-in-law in a proper spirit. For he felt like old Mr. Cobbledyke in that admirable novel by the authors of *Ready-Money Mortiboy*, that whoever married his daughter must be prepared to make settlements, and that the settlements must be such as Mr. Cobbledyke contemplated, only more suited to his own rank and position in life.

Then it occurred to him that after all there is better security in land and in iron fields and furnaces than in any professional prospects, however brilliant. So that in stopping this doubtful marriage he would be really doing his duty to Marcia, and acting as every father with a proper and indeed Christian sense of his duty ought to act.

And apparently he found comfort in these

reflections. It is astonishing with how little effort a thoroughly selfish man can persuade himself that he is doing his duty.

John Douglas had a quick temper, which, as he kept it under absolute control in the exercise of his profession, gave him the more trouble in private life. He left the terrace burning with a desire to kick the selfish old man the whole length of it. Indeed, Sir Hugo would hardly have stepped along so jauntily if he had had the least idea of what was passing in the young man's mind.

Clearly, however, there were two things for Douglas to do at once: one was to see Marcia for himself, and the other to arrange that his clerk should telegraph for him to return to London without delay. The latter piece of strategy only required a stroll down to the village. The former was more difficult, for where Marcia was at that moment he did not know, nor did he know of whom to inquire. So he sauntered about the house and grounds, waiting upon time for his chance.

At last he boldly went into the library and wrote Marcia his first letter to her. I am not going to reproduce this epistle, but I will say that it was a model. It told Marcia exactly and briefly what had occurred, and added that as Sir Hugo's consent had been refused in a manner that was evidently intended to be final, he wished her to know that he himself should wait patiently until the time came when she would have the right to decide for herself. He should return to town that day. It would be hardly likely that they would meet in London for some little time; but, he added, months slip away while you are counting days and hours, and it would not be many months before the time would come when they need never be parted again. He should like to write to her in the interval, but would not do so without her permission.

This letter he managed by some exercise of diplomacy to get conveyed to Marcia, and before many minutes, although to him they seemed innumerable, he received an answer sufficiently characteristic :—

"Do not leave the Towers until I have seen you.

"M. C."

And now, for every historian must be truthful, I have to record that John

Douglas, instead of doing anything un-
practical, such as kissing the letter, put it
most methodically into his note-case, which
he carried in an inner pocket, and then in
the spirit of a soldier going into action,
resolved to make certain of meeting Marcia
before the day was over.

He had not long to wait, and fortune
favoured him. Sir Hugo, feeling that a
small glass of brandy and curacoa would
restore his nerves and give a tone to his
system, went in quest of that most unwholesome but not unpleasant compound.
One of the servants, who was putting away
the plate, divined at once what was wanted
of him, and provided the necessary cordial
with a promptitude really wonderful. Sir
Hugo drank a glass of it on the spot,
and sipped a second deliberately. The

hour perhaps was early, but a footman in a large house is like a Club waiter in one most valuable quality—nothing ever allows him to be betrayed into astonishment.

I once saw an experiment tried upon a Club waiter to test this great truth. He was ordered to bring a large wine glass, brandy and chili vinegar, and saw about a gill of the mixture tossed off without moving a muscle of his features.

And let me add, *par paranthèse*, that if you have gone through the ice, or have come in positively cramped from a Scotch mist, a moderate dose of this especial compound is as good a " corpse-reviver " as you can select, and more wholesome than might be supposed.

While the excellent parent was thus occupied Douglas waited in the library.

The room was well chosen, it being at that moment entirely deserted. Nor had he long to wait. Before he had almost mechanically cast his eye down a column of the *Field*, Marcia came in, walked straight up to him, and held out her hand.

"I am sorry," she said, "that you are going. I suppose there is no help for it. But we shall meet again in London before long I hope."

This was refreshingly frank, as Douglas knew that Marcia in London hardly went out at all. She had given him, indeed, pretty much the same account of her daily life as that which I have given the reader.

What ought Douglas to have said? It is odd that at these precise junctures a clever man finds his power of exact expression hopelessly gone. But he looked

Marcia straight in the eyes, and took her hand, and said, "Good-bye. It is not for long."

"Not very long," she laughed, "but while it lasts we must wait. Meantime, do not imagine that I shall ever change. I have given you my promise, and I shall keep it."

"We must wait, I suppose," said Douglas.

"There is no help for it." This was prosaic, but it was about the only thing to be said.

Then Douglas, I grieve to say, degenerated into poetry, or to use the expressive phrase of Mr. Silas Wegg, "dropped into" it. On the little finger of his left hand was a diamond ring—a single brilliant in a perfectly plain hoop.

Opinions differ as to whether men ought

to wear jewelry or not. We know from classical authors that a Roman barrister in large practice used always to carry an immense ring, and flourish it at the jury. Juniors with a smaller practice used to hire a ring for the day, paste at that time not having been discovered or invented. A small diamond of the first water is perhaps permissible,—it is not like one of those obtrusive gems the size of a hazel nut, with which bill-discounters and meat salesmen and book-makers love to dazzle you.

Douglas took the ring, and slipped it on to the third finger of Marcia's left hand.

"The stone was my mother's," he said, "and she had it set for me the day I was called."

And then this bad man with true legal ingenuity equivocated, for he pretended to kiss the ring as if he were bidding it good-bye; and to kiss a ring on a lady's hand and nothing but the ring is a difficult task.

Marcia had no ring to give him in return. Things at times have a habit of going awkwardly. The diamond, of course, must not be taken off again, and under it lay her only other ornament, her mother's engaged ring.

"I cannot give you this," she said, touching it. "I am not going to take off the diamond, as that would be unlucky. Besides," she added, with a laugh that was earnest—for it is quite possible to laugh earnestly—"the ring you have given me was your mother's, and the little gold hoop was all that my own mother wore except her wedding ring for many years."

Douglas laughed merrily. "We must

not spoil luck," he said, and he kissed her hand again.

"But," continued Marcia, "I will send you a present, such as it is, before you leave the house." And then she drew herself up to her full height, held out her hand, and said, "I am going now, and you may write to me both here and at Sloane Street."

There are matter-of-fact elements in all incidents of life, and even after what had passed between them, it was a matter-of-fact and mechanical kind of thing for Douglas to open the door and bow once again over Marcia's hand as she passed out.

Next, what did he do? Being an Englishman, he walked to the fire and stirred it vigorously. Then he planted himself on the hearth-rug with his back to the mantel-piece. Did he think? Yes, he did;

and it was of nothing in particular, for he was too happy and, indeed, self-satisfied to think definitely. It is a singular thing that men seem to concentrate their ideas when they plant themselves on the hearth-rug, in its very centre, with their back to the fire. There is a philosophy in these things. Why does a man fold his arms when he has made up his mind? Why does he beat the devil's tattoo when he cannot quite make up his mind? Why does he look up when he is thinking of the future, and on the ground when he is thinking of the past?

There must be a reason for all these things. They are relics of our long-forgotten ancestry, and the act is unconscious on our own part—as unconscious as that of the dog who turns round three or four times before he finally lies down to sleep, and then the moment he has lain down heaves his chest and blows an immense respiration through his nostrils. His ancestors used to make themselves a little lair for the night in the grass or brushwood, and used to clear their nostrils with a deep blow, that even while asleep they might scent the advent of a possible enemy. Look at Mr. Darwin's learned remarks on the descent of man, and you will find it explained why, when a man gets into a passion, he draws back his lips and shows all his teeth.

John Douglas was still warming himself in this attitude when the expected telegram from his faithful clerk reached him. Blessed is the barrister's clerk that lieth for his master. Verily he shall not be disappointed of his reward when they say unto that master, "Learned brother, sit up higher."

Thus ran the mendacious missive—
"From Henry Jenkinson, Temple. To
John Douglas, Esquire, St. Austell Towers,
Oakshire. Consultation fixed specially.
Attorney General's to-morrow. Special fee.
Bedford Level improvements. Cookson,
Cookson, Goldsworthy, &c. View next day
if possible."

Here was a happy way out of difficulties.
Douglas dashed up-stairs, packed his port-
manteau, saw Lady St. Austell, and let the
telegram speak for itself, wrote a letter to
Lord St. Austell, and was soon on his way
to the station.

"One more or less will not be missed
in so big a house," he reflected. And then
he lit a cigar.

When he had fairly gone the servants
wondered among themselves at his liber-

ality. For there is honour of their own among servants, and you may safely trust your gratuities in a lump sum to one who is in authority among them.

In the train Douglas read the papers, for he had not the facts of the great Bedford Level case as yet before him, nor indeed was he ever likely to be troubled with them. Nor have I anything now to add except that he dined that evening at his club, and wrote a letter to Marcia, thanking her for the presents which he had received before he left the house. They were a small enamelled locket, and her own photograph with her signature.

I suppose there ought also to have been a lock of her hair, but for this he had not asked, and so she had not sent it. Perhaps he ought to have remembered to ask, only one forgets lesser matters on great and hurried occasions.

There are some things which men will never know about women, or women about men, and about these things there are pretty and almost pious fictions. Douglas ought, according to all rules, from those of chivalry down to our own day, to have lain awake all night thinking of Marcia. I have no hesitation in saying that he did nothing of the sort. He was not exactly in the humour for a theatre, but he played a game or two of whist at his club, and then went to bed and to sleep in the most matter-of-fact manner possible.

As for the great Bedford Level case, Lady St. Austell had forgotten its very name within a quarter of an hour, so he was never troubled afterwards with any awkward inquiries. But I think Mr. Jenkinson deserved credit for his ingenuity; and I have no doubt that if the Bedford Level or any other level had led to litigation, either litigant might have done worse than to have sent Douglas a heavy brief, with the pleasant subscription to his name, "With you the Attorney - General, Mr. Joshua Jawkins, Q.C., and Mr. Tugwell."

CHAPTER X.

MARCIA, when she left John Douglas, was crossing the hall with the intention of making her way to her own room and thinking. Edgar Allen Poe has gone so far as to say that you can always think best in the dark. You certainly can think best when you are alone, and I will positively defy any man to think if he knows that his meditations may be at any moment interrupted. This is why some wicked people find it so easy to think in church when the sermon has begun and the preacher has fairly settled down into his stride.

Marcia had almost gained the foot of the stairs when she encountered her estimable parent, who at once assumed his choicest air of affectionate sorrow. And I must say, in justice to Sir Hugo, that he was really on this occasion extremely grieved and pained. He had the misty idea I have before referred to, that he had been making great sacrifices for Marcia's welfare, that he had somehow devoted the best years of his life to her, and that the only return he had met was base ingratitude. Had he ever been compelled to earn a living, I think Sir Hugo would have made a very good first old gentleman, and there was now about him almost a touch of King Lear. He settled his features into an appropriate sadness, and there was something like a quiver in his voice, as if the words hung in his throat.

"Marcia," he said, "I wish you would put on your things and come for a little walk with me. The sun is tempting, and I feel a walk might do me good. Besides, my dear, I wish to speak to you."

Marcia, knowing perfectly well what was about to come, betrayed no symptom of emotion of any kind, not even of curiosity.

"Certainly, papa; I will get ready at once. Will you meet me here?"

"Very well, my dear. I will be here, let us say, in five minutes. You, I dare say, will be a little longer."

"I will hurry, papa," and Marcia ran upstairs; while Sir Hugo braced his nerves for what he knew would be the most awkward encounter of all with some French brandy, neat, for once, and wrapped himself up with the greatest care, as if he knew how precious was his own life to the world at large, and was determined not to run the slightest risk of even a cold.

His preparations were hardly completed when his daughter joined him in the hall, with a look in her eyes that distinctly said, "Gentlemen of the guard, fire first!" and entirely threw Sir Hugo off his balance.

"I hear, my dear child," he said, as they found themselves on the gravel side by side, "I hear with considerable astonishment from Mr. Douglas—a young man, I believe, of some ability, and I may even say promise—that you have consented to marry him, subject, I presume, to my approval."

"He asked me to marry him, papa, and I wished him to speak to you. He has told me what passed between you, and we are now going to wait until I am of age."

Sir Hugo did not exactly know how to meet this kind of answer. He was in much the position as a man who, having demanded an apology in the certainty of at once getting it, is told to go to a place not generally named and to get it there. What is a man to do with his own daughter when she distinctly lets him know that she is not afraid of him, and does not intend to obey him?

Perhaps Sir Hugo did the best thing under all the circumstances. He blew his nose, with a tinge of pathos in the performance.

"My dear child," he said (and this was

stagy and unwise. It was the very last kind of tack on which he should have started with Marcia), "my dear child, I confess I am deeply grieved and wounded. I have been, Marcia, a loving and tender parent to you. Since your dear mother's death you have been my one and only thought and care, and I confess that I expected some other return from you for all my devotion—some other return than ingratitude." And the man at this point gave way to the father, for the excellent old gentleman very nearly broke down.

Marcia remained silent, which was very annoying. Her father, of course, would have liked a scene, and in fact wanted it. There was much in his nature of a certain type of feminine cunning, and he had an idea that out of a real good scene he should

come with flying colours. Evidently, however, there was not to be a scene, so he
turned on the tremolo stop again.

"I am getting old, Marcia. Time is telling on me. I may be summoned at any
moment." (His look of resignation to the
decrees of Providence was inimitable.)
"Life has little left for me, and my years
will not be many. I promised your dearest
mother that I would watch over you, and
do my best to supply the irreparable loss
that fell upon you by her death. Day and
night, early and late, I have had your
welfare constantly in my mind. And I
should be neglecting the most sacred of all
duties if I did not make it the one object
of my solicitude to see your future secured
by a suitable marriage. I think, Marcia,
I have a right to expect that in this most

important matter of all you should not have acted without my approval or even my consent."

Marcia's answer was very short, and, like many short answers, was all the more effective.

"My dear papa," she said, "this is a matter in which I surely have the first right to an opinion. If I am to marry I shall be giving the whole of what is left of my life. My own life is as serious a matter to me as it can possibly be to you. And I cannot see why you should object to a marriage which would at once relieve you of all responsibility so far as I am concerned, and enable you to live as you have hitherto done, almost without being aware of my existence."

Now here Sir Hugo was puzzled. If he had been a man with any courage in him he would have told Marcia at once to go about her business, and would have taken the whole matter into his own hands. But selfish men are always cowards. They are haunted by the idea that they will have to do something, or to give something.

The story of Iphigenia comes down to our own day, only that fathers do not stab their own daughters with a butcher's knife. Otherwise, all the rest is true. Sir Hugo could not have stabbed any living thing. The mere sight of blood, or even the smell of it, would have unhinged him for at least a fortnight. But he was none the less resolute in having his own way. It is curious how many men mislead themselves.

A man who has made his living for some years over the billiard table discovers that his wife has musical ability, and it at once occurs to him that she ought to go upon the Music Hall stage, and to earn an income sufficient to support the entire family. Nor is this mistaken point of view confined to men. I have known men—a man, let me say—whose wife has shaken him up in the morning by the collar of his nightgown, and yelled in his ears, "Why do you not get up? Why do you not write poetry like Lord Byron, or a history like Gibbon? Why do you not write a play like the Private Secretary, or the Candidate? Why do you not—— ?" It is really too pitiful to follow this kind of argument.

But Sir Hugo, unhappily, had made up his mind that Marcia's marriage was to be for his own special and particular benefit. It is unpleasant to study morbid anatomy. It is equally unpleasant to follow the

reasoning of a thoroughly selfish man.   But
Sir Hugo's reasoning was of this kind.

"I have treasured the girl as the apple of
my eye since her mother's death.   I have
been the best, the most kind, the most
generous, and the most indulgent of fathers.
I have sacrificed my life for her."   Now
this was most entirely and strictly untrue.
For Sir Hugo had all the vices which were
possible for a man of his age, and indulged
in them, not without an air of resignation,
as if he considered that he were by his
brilliant example keeping younger men
out of mischief, and teaching them to
know the ropes.   You would find him
in places commonly considered dangerous,
or, to say the least, not quite reputable.
His first words with you allayed your
suspicions.

"Odd it is how little these places alter. It is just as I remember it thirty years ago. But it is tiresome. Let us have a brandy and soda. Not here, for Heaven's sake. Let us go to the Club."

These remarks usually got rid of the person to whom they were addressed. Sir Hugo was of course very well known about London. But is it not a fact, that if a man is six feet in height, with grey hair and a moustache to match, if he dresses well, if he is always absolutely sober, if he pays his bets, and if he is not suspected of sharp play, either at cards or billiards, he is, as a rule, accepted as the ideal of an English gentleman? Should he spend a couple of guineas on his supper, no man asks whether his wife and children are starving on bread and butter in Pentonville. Were I to write

a learned book on success in life,—success
inspired by no lofty motives—I should lay
down for a young man the following rules :—

1. Never forget a friend or forgive an
enemy.

2. Never let anybody know anything
about you, unless you can turn the confidence to your own advantage.

3. Always live well and dress well.   But
dine off a crust sooner than have a spot of
grease on your hat.

4. Never make any place too hot to hold
you.   Always let it be possible for you to
come back ; pay up, and take your old
position.

5. Recollect that the older you grow the
wiser you become, and the more venerable
you look.   If a man has a venerable look,
and also knows the world as a wild fowler

knows his marshes, he will find the supply of fools infinite.

6. Fools are like wild fowl. They have too much feather on them, and have never heard of decoys or of goose-shot.

These are a more or less complete set of commandments, although no doubt judicious additions might easily be made to them. There is a much simpler rule of life suitable for the smallest boy. Never tell a lie. Never take a blow. Never prig.

A boy needs no bigger catechism than this. As he becomes older his relations with the world become more complex, and his responsibilities more onerous.

Captain Cuttle used to observe that the bearings of an observation lay in the application of it. Blows are out of the question for a lady. Prigging was out of all question for Marcia. Her sole duty under this table of three commandments was to tell the truth. This was a duty she could undertake fearlessly. It would save an immense amount of trouble in this very troublesome world if people would only tell the truth. A falsehood serves your purpose for the minute, but it comes back to you ten years afterwards with infinite punishment in its train. Truth is very cheap and very short. Also it entails no strain on the imagination.

Now Marcia had told her father the exact truth with regard to her relations with Douglas—neither above it, below it, before it, nor behind it. There are some people who are constitutionally incapable of a lie. They simply cannot tell it. Marcia was one of these.

I have thus indicated the various points

of view taken by Sir Hugo and Marcia of what really ought to have been a very simple question. It would have been the simplest question in the world if Sir Hugo had not complicated it by his own selfishness, and have aggravated his selfishness by pretending that it was paternal solicitude. Let me sum up the points as they are at present at issue.

Sir Hugo wants his daughter to marry a man with a large house and many servants, where he can live as a pensioner without causing sufficient friction to make the suggestion possible that his visit has been unduly protracted. I really believe that if you say as little and do as little as possible, except at the right time and to the right persons—if, that is to say, you do not put yourself *en evidence*,—you can stay in a big house, if you have a shadow of a claim upon its owner, for almost as long as you please.

There are artifices over this stratagem. You must have breakfast in bed, and limit it to toast and cocoa. You must look in at lunch towards its finish. You must take especial care to make yourself conversation-ally useful at dinner. For to be useful is a more humble task than to be brilliant, or even ornamental. The highest gift you can possess is that of gliding into the con-versation and diverting it into a channel which permits everybody to talk. You yourself need then only nod approval. This, however, is a very rare accomplish-ment. The rarest of all is that of talking up to the biggest man at the table, and coaxing him into expansion, until he tells

you, all of you, how he was flogged at
Eton. Few men have the tact or the
nerve for this.

The second point is that Sir Hugo wants
that during the remainder of his life his
daughter shall not trouble him. It would
be a dreadful thing, for instance, if she
were to marry a government clerk or a
young barrister, and her husband were to
die, and she were to come back to him
with a couple of children. Sir Hugo hated
children of all sorts, looking on them as
things that get in your way, and divert
women from attentions to which you are
entirely and indefeasibly entitled. And he
would have hated unprovided-for descend-
ants most of all.

The third and last point is that Sir Hugo,
having cherished and nurtured the seed of

hope planted in his bosom by Lady St. Austell, has determined that, *per fas aut nefas*, his daughter shall marry one or other of those eligible young men—Lord Norwich or Mr. Davidson.

Marcia, on her part, has equally made up *her* mind to marry John Douglas. Nothing shall come between them, she is firmly resolved. This young woman came to St. Austell Towers perfectly heart-whole. She met Douglas as I have described, and liking him from the first, soon had her heart filled with a warmer feeling, which the present difficulties with which the two are threatened have only served to increase. She is quite prepared for the worst, which after all cannot be very terrible, for she stands in no fear of her father, and will decline in a most uncompromising manner to be bullied into compliance with his wishes.

"My dear child," said Sir Hugo, after receiving Marcia's home-thrust, "if you will be good enough to abstain from being rude, and to listen to me for five minutes, I think that we shall probably come to the conclusion that we have been of the same mind after all. I can quite understand your finding Sloane Street dull, and becoming tired of the society of the Fräulein, and wanting to *ranger* yourself in life, and so accepting the first decent offer. I have not the faintest objection to your marrying. In fact, it is the only thing for you to do. But what I do object to, and most strongly, is that you should throw yourself away upon the first comer, when with your beauty and my influence you might command the most brilliant marriage."

"I love Mr. Douglas, papa, and I shall marry him."

"Great heavens! grant me patience!" gasped Sir Hugo. "Are you aware that there are at present two millionaires in the house, either of whom you can have for the asking? Lady St. Austell is my informant. I need not say that she could have no object in deceiving me."

"I am not aware of the fact, papa; and if even it were so, I have promised Mr. Douglas that I will marry him, and I shall keep my word."

"I believe you have gone mad, Marcia. At any rate you will soon drive me so. Listen for one minute. There is young Norwich head over ears in love with you.

Every one can see it.   He may propose at
any moment; at least, if he does not hear
of this tomfoolery with Douglas.   And if
you prefer it, there is Mr. Davidson the
ironmaster, who would—Lady St. Austell,
mark you, is my authority, and she takes a
most motherly interest in you—be only
too charmed to marry you, and settle a
hundred and fifty thousand pounds upon
you into the bargain.   And with chances
like these, and brilliant prospects like these,
you propose to throw yourself away upon an
adventurer like Douglas."

"Mr. Douglas is no adventurer, papa.
You would not dare to tell him so to his
face.   Why do so behind his back?   I
told Lady St. Austell, or at least let her
clearly understand, that I could never look
upon Lord Norwich in any other light than

that of a friend. I could never become really attached to him. And as for Mr. Davidson, I have not spoken half-a-dozen words to him. I am not to be bought and sold to suit your convenience, papa, or the convenience of any one else. I have made my mind up, and I tell you, for once and for all, that it is utterly useless to attempt to shake my resolve."

"If you are insane enough to abandon such a future as I have mapped for you for such a shabby existence as you contemplate I have no argument left to use. I shall, however, ask Lady St. Austell to reason with you. She may possibly have more weight with you than I. At all events, you will not be able to accuse her of self-interest. I am very hurt at your wicked and unfeeling conduct, and also at your cruel and unjust insinuations with regard to myself. Now, if you please, we will return home."

"Very well, papa; just as you like."

People may say that Marcia did not do her duty as a daughter. They may add that she was ignorant of the world. I venture to differ from them on both points.

In the first place, Marcia's marriage was a thing that, as she said, concerned herself more than her father. Sir Hugo had no right to entangle it in an undercurrent of ways and means leading to his own comfort.

A girl is not bound to marry an oyster merchant to whom she objects because her father is fond of oysters, and is anxious to get them at trade price, or even for nothing. And I for one can see no

P 2

difference between oysters and other lesser ends to which selfishness looks. It may be oysters, or good claret, or anything else. Anyhow, Sir Hugo wanted to sell his daughter that he might live more luxuriously, and, in fact, after his own ideas of comfort. And this was very wicked on the part of Sir Hugo; it was also very unchristian; it was worse than very unchristian, for it was very selfish; it was worse than selfish, for it was almost ungentlemanly. Even Jephthah did not propose to sell his daughter for a daily mess of potage.

But Sir Hugo felt that he was getting older. He had lived in London all his life; he had never really felt the wholesome stimulus of family affection. There are many such men. It is idle to attempt to bring them to a sense of their duty. "Sir," said a billiard-marker once to the writer of these pages, naming a man pretty well known at the time in London society, "if you were to kick that man down a passage a mile long in which there wasn't room for him to turn round, I don't believe that he could run straight."

It was Sir Hugo's chief fault that he could not run straight.

CHAPTER XI.

THE first thing that Sir Hugo did after luncheon was to secure a *tête-à-tête* with Lady St. Austell, into whose sympathetic ears the thwarted parent poured a recital of all his woes. I say "sympathetic," because although her ladyship did not entirely agree with the view that Sir Hugo took of the matter, nevertheless, having promised to assist in the matrimonial campaign, and having indeed commenced operations already, she felt more than a kindly interest in the result.

And, as I have already hinted, Lady St.

Austell liked Sir Hugo. She had in reality only seen the best side of him, and recollected what he was in the old days before he left the army, and when she herself was within an ace of becoming Lady Conyers. Of the real Sir Hugo she had not an idea. On the contrary, she gave him credit for absolute disinterestedness with regard to his daughter's future, and believed that he was actuated by the best and sincerest motives.

"I will speak to her to-morrow," said Lady St. Austell. "After all, if she insists on marrying Mr. Douglas it is not such a bad match. He is very clever and steady, and is sure to get on. His family is an excellent one. St. Austell has known them all his life, and indeed was a great friend of Mr. Douglas's father."

"All this is no doubt true, dear Lady St. Austell. But I should question whether Mr. Douglas has a farthing more than he earns. These young barristers are all alike. What settlements could he make? None, of course. It would be a most precarious marriage, and it would be wicked on my part to sanction it or countenance it in any way. I couldn't do it, indeed I could not."

"Very well, Sir Hugo, there is something in what you say, and I will talk to Marcia. But I warn you that young ladies of the present day have an awkward habit of making up their minds for themselves, and if she is really in love I much doubt whether I shall have any success."

"It's an awful responsibility!" said Sir Hugo. "But nothing will make me swerve from my manifest duty."

The next morning after breakfast Lady St. Austell invited Marcia to come to her boudoir. "I dare say, my dear child, you will guess why I want to speak to you."

"Yes, I think I know, Lady St. Austell."

"Now, Marcia," said her ladyship after they had sat down, "I have promised your papa to have a little talk with you. You see, my child, you necessarily know very little of the world, and you have no mother to advise you. So if you will let me, I will try and supply her place, and will act towards you as if you were my own."

Now Lady St. Austell, to do her justice, was perfectly sincere in all this, and her manner of saying it convinced Marcia of the fact, so that a feeling of affection and gratitude sprang up in the girl's heart.

"Thank you, Lady St. Austell, I know

you are my friend. I will listen to everything you say."

"That's right, dear. Your papa tells
me that you have engaged yourself to Mr.
Douglas who was staying here. I suppose
that this is the case."

"Yes, Lady St. Austell."

"I fear, dear, that neither of you have
been very prudent. You see, Mr. Douglas
has no fortune. He is a most estimable
man; I wish a few more of the present
generation were like him. But he has little
or nothing but that for which he works.
Suppose that he were to fall ill, and his
income thereby cease. What would you
both do? You see he is too young to
have had time to save any money. You
have none, and your papa could allow you
little or nothing."

"I should not mind roughing it," said Marcia.

"No, my dear, perhaps not. But marriages such as the one you are contemplating often end in something worse than roughing it. Believe me, that when the pinch comes, as it too often does, love flies away, and a feeling very like aversion takes its place. The man recognizes that many of the petty troubles and annoyances which he has to bear would never have come upon him had it not been for his marriage; and the woman cannot fail to realize how much happier her life might have been had she only made a more prudent choice, and taken the advice of those who knew the world better than she. Then an estrangement takes place. It may be gradual or it may be sudden, but in any case it is certain, and thus two lives are marred."

"But Mr. Douglas seems such a sensible man. Do you think he would want me to marry him if he did not see his way clearly as to the future?"

"A man in love, my child, is little better than a fool. He never considers the consequences of what he is doing. Mr. Douglas is in all ordinary affairs a most sensible and keen-witted young man. But the fact is, your beauty has turned his head, and he is proposing to do the most foolish thing in the world, both with regard to his interest and your own."

"I shouldn't like Mr. Douglas to injure his future for my sake," said Marcia.

"I am sure of that, dear. No good-hearted or proper-minded girl could wish that."

"I like Mr. Douglas very much. I never liked any one so much before, and the prospect of being his wife has made me happier than I have been for a long time. But I would give all this up if you are certain of what you say, dear Lady St. Austell. I will be quite frank with you. I would not do this for my father's sake. I would only do it for Mr. Douglas's own sake."

"You are taking a very sensible and proper view of the matter, Marcia. If I was conscientiously able to further this marriage I would do so, and that too in spite of your father's objections, if I thought they were wrong or unfounded.

But for both your sakes I cannot do this. And I strongly advise you to write to Mr. Douglas and tell him what conclusion you have arrived at. Or, if you prefer it, I will do so for you. What do you say, Marcia?"

"Very well, Lady St. Austell, you write, please," replied Marcia, bursting into tears and hurrying from the room.

"I don't like this," said Lady St. Austell to herself. "But I suppose Sir Hugo was right. After all, it would have been a most imprudent marriage. And I am certain that Norwich will propose to her. But I never thought I should manage her so easily. I wonder whether she is really in love with Douglas. I do indeed."

*   *   *   *   *   *

"*St. Austell Towers,*
"*Oct. 22nd, 18—*

"Dear Mr. Douglas,

"I never felt greater difficulty in commencing a letter, although what I have to say is after all very plain.

"To come to the point at once, Sir Hugo Conyers has told me of your engagement to his daughter, and of his strong disapproval of such a step. Now, dear Mr. Douglas, I will be perfectly frank with you, and I must say at once that I think Sir Hugo is right. Lord St. Austell and I have the very highest opinion of you, and I have not hesitated to express our feelings towards you in discussing this matter with Sir Hugo. But you have no fortune, and you are entirely dependent on your profession for your income. Marcia

Conyers is a portionless girl, and it would be, in my opinion, the height of imprudence for any two young people to marry under such circumstances.

"I have told Marcia this, and I now repeat it to you. In the advice I have given Marcia, who has no mother of her own to consult, I have considered you quite as much as her.

"And I must now tell you that Marcia, in spite of her evidently strong attachment to you, sees things in this light, and has commissioned me to write to you, and beg you to consider everything at an end. Believe me, my dear friend, it is best that it should be so.

"Lord St. Austell and I take the greatest interest in your career, and we shall both be glad to hear good news of you, and to see you here whenever you can find time to run away from town.

"With kindest regards, believe me,

"Your sincere friend,

"EMILY ST. AUSTELL.

"P.S. Marcia has just sent me your ring, which she has begged me to return. You will receive it by the same post as this letter."

"My dearest Marcia," said Sir Hugo to his daughter the next day, "Lady St. Austell has been telling me of your sensible conduct. You now see, my dear, that in refusing to sanction your marriage with Mr. Douglas I was only acting in your interest, and—"

"Papa, if you wish me to retain one spark of affection for you you will not speak to me again on this subject. And what is more, I decline to discuss it with you."

"Very well, my dear," replied Sir Hugo, perfectly satisfied at having gained his point, "we will say no more about it. After all, I dare say that you are right. Will you come for a little stroll? No? So sorry. It is a lovely morning, and the birds are singing, and the sun is shining, and all nature seems to be joyful and full of contentment. A wonderful thing nature! When you have children of your own you will know what it is. Go and enjoy yourself, my darling; you are looking a little paler than I altogether like. Dear me, how like your mother you are getting. It is positively wonderful! Good-bye, my sweet, good-bye."

And good Sir Hugo somehow gravitated again towards the billiard room. Curaçoa such as that to be had at the Towers was beyond his reach in London.

Marcia for her part chose some stout boots, a long thick cloak, a hat of the kind known as "the deerstalker," and a somewhat uncompromising umbrella, and sallied out into the air. It was a crisp, cheery day; the ground rang pleasantly under her feet, and the blood began to move in her veins and bring the colour to her cheeks. All the manly element in her nature seemed to assert itself. For a strong nature there is a positive pleasure in defying and facing the worst troubles.

She had not gone far before she became aware of the approach of Lord Norwich, who it is charitably to be hoped had been

Q 2

told in which direction to find her. On any other assumption the hopeless bewilderment of this young man would have been ludicrous. His lordship blundered into conversation much in the fashion of a fairly good skater making his first fifty or hundred strokes after half-a-dozen blank winters. He remarked that it was cold, and safely added that there was always good snipe shooting in cold weather, a fact of which Marcia was not aware. From snipe he diverged to figure-skating, and finding that Marcia could not execute the outside edge backwards, expressed his opinion that she ought to make herself mistress of that accomplishment, which he explained only required nerve.

In Canada the ladies acquired it while young, and were absolutely perfect in it.

Marcia expressed a regret more or less sincere at her inability to achieve the outside edge either forward or backwards, and her readiness to study it upon the first opportunity.

His lordship next ascertained that she was fond of horses, but could neither drive nor ride. And ultimately, having exhausted these and some other similar topics of interest, he expressed his emphatic conviction, with all his schoolboy good-nature, that it was "a shame" for her to be unequal to these things, which were all useful and extremely pleasant, and needed nothing more for their acquisition than practise combined with the necessary determination.

It was impossible to be angry with this young man; his good nature was as evident as his sincerity. He amused Marcia, and to a certain extent pleased her, for she was quite sufficiently human to enjoy a sincere compliment.

And so Lord Norwich, in sporting phraseology, warmed up and settled down into his work. He should like, he told Marcia, above all things to have the high pleasure of being her tutor in the various accomplishments that they had discussed, and more particularly in the art of tandem driving, which he explained was to all other forms of driving what tennis is to other games with ball, and as far superior to four-in-hand as is billiards to bagatelle. And having thus stood for a minute or two on the bank, Lord Norwich boldly took his header.

"I'm not a good hand at saying what

I mean, Miss Conyers," he began. "Talking is one of the things they leave out in our education. But what I want to say, if you will allow me, is, that you would make me the proudest and happiest man in the world if you would take me as you find me. I would do every mortal thing I could to make you happy. I won't talk about gratifying all your wishes. That goes of course. But I would do anything and everything to show you how sincere I am in what I am saying. And I would live where you liked—in London, or in the country, or abroad; and perhaps, if there is any place you particularly liked, you wouldn't mind choosing a house there, or having one built to your own fancy, and having it for your own, to go to whenever you pleased, or wanted to be quiet. One

does not always care for visitors, and I
think all ladies like some sort of hermi-
tage of their own. I know my mother
did. And "—he laughed—"my father
never dared so much as pass the lodge
gates without her permission."

Here at last was the nettle to be grasped.
Marcia laid hold of it firmly.

She waited a minute or two, and then
said, "All this is very kind of you, Lord
Norwich,—kinder still because I am sure
you mean it. I had better be quite frank
with you. It is always best to tell the
truth. I cannot possibly do as you ask,
for the very best of reasons. I am engaged to nobody else; but there is some
one of whom I have been very fond,
although I shall never marry him. I could
not honestly marry any other man. That

is all, Lord Norwich. Let us forget this
morning, and let us always be the best
of friends. I do not mind telling you "—
and here her voice rang pleasantly—"that
I should like to always reckon you among
my few friends."

Lord Norwich, in an account of this
interview to his dearest and closest old
friend and brother officer, emphatically
declared that the young lady completely
"bottled" him. The phrase may not be
exactly an elegant one, but its native sim-
plicity is complete.

What ought a nobleman and ex-guards-
man to say when he is completely
"bottled"? Pretty much, I suppose,
what Lord Norwich did. He told Marcia
he was honoured by her confidence, and
would respect it. He expressed a hope

that she might perhaps change her determination, and said something simple and
to the point about his own resolve to
wait.   He would wait for her, he told
her, for years, and in the interval he
supposed they would meet occasionally.
And then, being a sensible young man,
he said nothing more, but began to talk
about what may be best described as
" anything."

With commendable adroitness he allowed
Marcia to pick the way, and somehow the
way led them back to the house, at which
when they arrived they were really upon
most excellent terms with one another.
Why should they not have been ? Lord
Norwich was one of the best and most
warm-hearted of young men, and Marcia
felt this. Marcia herself had been straight-

forward, and Lord Norwich respected her for it. How very much easier and happier life would become at once if we would only tell each other the exact truth as these two young people had just done.

What was now the result of the whole thing? A marriage prevented which might possibly have been wearisome, and if so, certainly unhappy, and instead of it a firm and honest friendship cemented. For a good man the friendship of a good woman, and for a good woman the friendship of a good man is invaluable. It is one of the few things in this life worth having.

So both Marcia and Lord Norwich thought and felt as they shook hands heartily under the portico before passing into the hall.

CHAPTER XII.

ON receiving and reading Lady St. Austell's letter—he read it carefully two or three times—Douglas put the document into his pocket, lit a cigar, and walked leisurely to his Club by way of the Embankment.

At the Club he wrote a couple of letters, each very brief and pronouncedly business-like. One was to Lady St. Austell, the other to Marcia. That to Lady St. Austell was little more than an acknowledgment of her letter to himself, concluding with the interesting information that he was now once again hard at work, for which his visit to St. Austell Towers had made him fully fit, and in fact almost impatient. That to Marcia was, as lawyers used to say, *in hac verbâ*.

> " *Oxford and Cambridge Club,*
> " *October* 30*th*, 18—.

"Dear Miss Conyers,

"You are of course aware that I have heard from Lady St. Austell. Pray consider yourself perfectly and entirely free from any kind of pledge or promise you may ever have given me.

"It is only due to myself to state that I am not an adventurer, and could have sufficiently provided both for your present and for any possible future. This, I hope, you will believe, or if you doubt it, you can easily satisfy yourself when you return to London.

"I once had your good opinion, and I should not like you to think that I was altogether unworthy it.

"Yours sincerely,

"JOHN DOUGLAS."

These letters finished and posted, Mr. Douglas, having nothing else to do, strolled round to some very well-known livery stables in Piccadilly where (I had forgotten to mention the fact) he kept his horse. A brisk trot to Richmond with a canter in the Park will fit you admirably afterwards for a plain dinner, not at the Star and Garter, which is practically closed in October, but a certain good old-fashioned house down in the town, where you can get a beef-steak with mashed potatoes and onions and a pickled walnut, with a bottle of sound port and a good cigar.

John Douglas was a simple man, liking old-fashioned houses and good plain cookery. This is the true stoic philosophy, the net outcome of which is that those, after all, who expect the least in this world go to the certain way to get the most.

And then, after a few compliments exchanged with the host, Douglas let out his stirrup-leathers a couple of holes and jogged back to town at that most delightful of all paces to any man who can ride—a steady covert trot. All of which things may seem prosaic, and no doubt are, but ninety-nine per cent. of life is prose of the most substantial and unvarnished kind. And it is fortunate for us that this should

be the case. Else a man with any brains
would at once flare down in the socket as
a taper does when we plunge it into a jar
of oxygen.

When Douglas found himself again in
his chambers he began to think over things.
This was only natural, and in no way a
symptom of weakness. He had been harder
hit than he cared to own even to himself,
although of course the whole thing was
now over. And he had been insulted into
the bargain by the veriest old Polonius
that ever trod the boards of real life—only
that Polonius was merely an old driveller,
well meaning in his stupid way, and wholly
unselfish. Now no one could say as much
as this in favour of Sir Hugo. And, into
the bargain, he had been patronized—a
thing that no man likes at any time, and

is doubly irritating when the patronage is absolutely uncalled-for and offered with superfluous fuss and rustle of condescension.

And, as all these things recurred to him, he in his own mind heartily and emphatically cursed the whole business from beginning to end, and vowed with great fervour that he would never again make such a fool of himself.

This, of course, was wholly unnecessary, as he had not made a fool of himself at all. There is all the difference in the world between making a fool of yourself and being fooled by other people. The last is a thing that may happen to the strongest of men, especially if he be of a generous disposition.

He thus then, as it were, drew a heavy line down these pages of his diary to show that they were finally settled and done with, and so closed the book with what in metaphor I will call a slam.

After all, the best and the fullest portion of his life was still before him, and there was no reason upon earth why he should not use it wisely and enjoy it thoroughly. There were no skeletons in his cupboard, and if a man without a skeleton in his cupboard cannot live happily and add to the happiness of other people, there must be some extraordinary defect in his constitution.

There being no such defect in the constitution of John Douglas, he, in a matter-of-fact way worthy of the oldest coasting skipper that ever yet trod deck, turned in, and was almost immediately wrapped in that sound sleep which we are taught to believe is the peculiar privilege of the just.

*   *   *   *   *   *

At St. Austell Towers his letters produced very much the effect he had intended they should.

Sir Hugo was glad that the thing was over, a result which he put down entirely to his own diplomacy, and upon which he proportionately plumed himself. Lady St. Austell was not a little nettled, but disposed in a friendly way to make allowances. She could not get it out of her head that both Douglas and Marcia were very young people who were all the better for a little sound advice given at the proper moment, and in a friendly manner.

There was once a benevolent old Scotch dame who expressed her conviction of the devil that he would be "nae the waur for a guid talking to." In a similar spirit of broad philanthropy her ladyship felt that Douglas had had his "talking to," and entertained a firm hope that it had done him good.

Marcia, with all her strength, was fairly broken down; and I do not know that I can add anything to these two words by any sort of expansion. All she could see before her was a life as dull and wearisome as the past, and with nothing in it like the little pleasures of her childhood and girlhood under the genial Fräulein to relieve its horrible monotony.

This is a crooked world, in which things go crookedly and perversely. Had there been at St. Austell Towers a single person with any observation, common sense, and moral courage—any one of such genuine

metal as that grand old lady, Miss Betsy
Trotwood—and who would have acted as
Marcia's friend, this miserable tangle would
have been seen and cut through. Mrs.
Jane Pontifex with her own " flap-doodle
and fudge" would have settled it in a
moment. Half, and more than half, the
unpleasantness in this world is due to moral
cowardice.

But the wretched Sir Hugo was not
yet out of his troubles. The full extent
of his misery was still unknown to him.
I think if ever any person in this world got
something like a share of the punishment
he deserved, it was that estimable father
when Lady St. Austell had to break to
him the terrible intelligence that Marcia
had actually so far forgotten her duty,
and everything else which a right-minded

young woman ought to hold most sacred, as to positively refuse the coronet which that really excellent and genial young man, Lord Norwich, had laid at her feet.

At first he refused altogether to believe the thing. It was too monstrous. It was out of the question. Then when he found that he had got to believe it, he worked himself into a passion which would have brought a man of less methodical and temperate habits dangerously near the verge of apoplexy.

He felt that he should like to shake Marcia, and lock her up in her room, and feed her upon bread of affliction and water of affliction for a good week or so.

He almost lamented that even stronger measures were not possible. Besides, he could not help seeing that he was left

in an awkward position as towards Lord
Norwich himself. Lord Norwich, he argued,
would think that he had been made a
fool of, and would be correspondingly
angry.

Now to such men as Sir Hugo the
anger of a peer in the position of Lord
Norwich is something more than a serious
thing. It is a very terrible matter indeed.
It may ruin him for life, or for so much
of life as he has left.

Sir Hugo, after all, was very ignorant
of the world as it now is—as ignorant
indeed as was that most profound scholar,
Dean Gaisford of Christ Church.

There came one day to Dean Gaisford
a young man who had taken a double
first, and who informed the learned editor
of Suidas (a most uncommonly useless

author) that he intended to resign his tutorship and to go to the Bar.

"To go to London," said the Dean doubtfully. "And how, sir, do you propose to succeed in London?"

The young man thus brought to book replied modestly that he had a small income, and he hoped reasonably fair abilities. The Dean laughed in his face. "Go to London if you like, sir," he said. "Of course I cannot stop you. But take my advice. Never mind your abilities, but attach yourself, if you can, to some person of position, and make yourself useful to him."

Perhaps the Dean in those days was not altogether wrong. He would most certainly be wrong now, when hardly a minister except the Lord Chancellor has any patronage at his disposal, and even that most august of State officials dare hardly perpetrate a downright job lest the profession should prove too strong for him.

Patronage has now practically become a public trust, and its exercise is jealously scrutinized even in that most Conservative of services—Her Majesty's.

Of all this, as of much else that had been going on during the latter years of his life, Sir Hugo was seriously and profoundly ignorant, and if you had told him that without powerful private friends behind him, John Douglas would certainly become a Judge, and very possible Lord Chief Justice, he would charitably have put the statement down to your inexperience.

Sir Hugo, accordingly, resolved to lie in wait for Lord Norwich, to bring all his

diplomacy to bear upon that young gentleman, to plead all kinds of excuses for
Marcia—wilfulness, bewilderment, anything
you please—and so, in his own way, to
bring matters to a happy issue.

First of all he had a stormy interview
with his daughter, in which, I regret to say,
he used unseemly and indeed almost un-
clubable language.   Then he extracted such
final words of consolation and advice as he
could from Lady St. Austell, before whom
he nervously paraded himself, like some
raw recruit under the inspection by a
general of more than average strength of
character and power of expression.   Then
he fortified himself, according to his usual
custom, with his favourite curaçoa and
brandy, and then he pulled himself together,
drew himself up to his full height, and went

at once in quest of Lord Norwich, lest his courage, now fairly screwed to the sticking-point, should in any way desert him.

Lord Norwich was easily found, and received Sir Hugo most courteously. He knew him to be a worthless, selfish man, and felt an almost pitying contempt for the game which his common sense had now thoroughly seen through.

But he was too much a gentleman to show anything of this to a man so much older than himself, and who happened also to be Marcia's father. So he received Sir Hugo, and listened to what he had to say, with every courtesy. Sir Hugo, of course, made a long story of the matter, during which he managed to talk an infinite deal of nothing, until Lord Norwich, from being amused, became bored, and from being bored felt strongly disposed to let himself become angry and to show it.

He was a simple young man, as I have said, who hated to have a fuss made about himself. However, he listened patiently.

With needless prolixity and iteration, Sir Hugo set out that he was deeply distressed and humiliated; that he had never been so distressed before in his life; that he could only ascribe his daughter's extraordinary conduct to caprice, and perhaps ignorance; that he had spoken to her himself very seriously, and as he hoped a father ought to speak under such astonishing circumstances; that Lady St. Austell herself had most kindly undertaken to see Marcia and to reason with her as her own dear mother—and here out came the tear, and after it the pocket-handkerchief to chase it

—would have done herself had she only
been spared; that he was very unhappy,
but had great faith in Lady St. Austell,
who was known to Marcia as his best and
oldest friend, and as almost a second mother
to herself.

And having reached this point, he was
pumped out and collapsed feebly. These
felicitous sporting phrases are the only ones
I know in which to convey the situation.

Lord Norwich, to Sir Hugo's utter horror
and dismay, took the matter quite cheerfully, and in a most practical and business-
like manner.

"I assure you, Sir Hugo," he said, "that
I entertain the most sincere admiration for
Miss Conyers, who has treated me in this
matter with the greatest straightforward-
ness. I am also sensible how much I shall

owe both to Lady St. Austell and to your-self for your kind offices. But I hardly anticipate that they will end as you expect, and I almost doubt if I should be doing the right thing in again forcing myself, or even appearing to force myself, upon your daughter. She has given me the simplest and very best reasons—reasons against which nothing could be urged, and which I was absolutely bound to respect—for her decision. I regret it deeply, but for my own part I do not see how it is to be helped. My own feelings towards Miss Conyers are entirely unchanged. They are, in fact, stronger than ever. But I should be simply doing a wrong thing if I made myself a party in any way to forcing her inclinations, and I ought to add that I have no intention of doing so."

How easy it is to be honest if you have only the requisite amount of courage, and how simple a way honesty is out of every possible difficulty! The frank avowal of Lord Norwich came upon Sir Hugo with all the dash and force of a waterspout. An American backwoodsman, using his own tongue, would have termed it a "slockdologer," and he would have been perfectly right.

Sir Hugo, however, being a man callous by this time, and not easily shamed, had no intention of being put off in this manner. Perhaps, his ready brain saw at once, the marriage might be arranged after all. Many a ship has ultimately been launched which has two or three times stuck obstinately in the stocks. Marcia no doubt had a temper of her own. But if you

bully, and pester, and bore, and cajole, and
entreat a woman from morning to night,
alternating between the methods, you may
ultimately get your way. Anyhow the one
thing to be done, clearly, was to gain time.
So Sir Hugo endeavoured to diplomatize,
and to tide matters over.

I will not inflict his harangue upon my
readers. It was a sort of dying wriggle, and
occupied so much time that before it was
concluded Lord Norwich had so far forgotten the amenities of life as to sit with
his hands deeply thrust into his trousers
pockets, and to attentively contemplate the
tips of his boots.

"Give 'em line," he afterwards explained
when describing the interview. "Give 'em
line. Wait till they are blown. If you in-
terrupt them they get their second wind,

and the whole thing has to be gone over again."

So Sir Hugo ran himself out a second time, and then remained more or less breathless, and evidently of opinion that there was no more to be said. This is a habit many people have when they have finished what they have got to say themselves. Lord Norwich, first waiting for some twenty or thirty seconds of courtesy then took up his parable.

"I am young, Sir Hugo," he said, "and perhaps not very bright, but I know a thing or two. I know when a lady means what she says, and wishes you once and for all to understand that she means it. It is open to me, of course, to tell you plumply that Miss Conyers has refused me once, and that I do not intend to subject myself

to the unpleasant experience of being refused again. That would be rude on my
part, and it would be most unfair to Miss
Conyers, who has behaved very handsomely.
I have had my answer, and I have taken
it, and I have no present intention of
troubling Miss Conyers again. I think I
said before that we parted on the best
of terms, and with the best possible
understanding."

Checkmate! Sir Hugo trotted out a
few sentences, always feeling it due to
himself, to his age, to his position in
society, and to a number of other things,
to have the last word. He had the last
word, or rather, the last hundred or so of
words, which it would have been unkind to
check, and then, as accountants would say,
the books were closed.

Sir Hugo "doddered" off at random. Lord Norwich went out into the open air. If there is one thing which more than another lets light upon a man's character, it is his behaviour at the very moment that the crisis is over.

When the jury returned into court with their verdict of guilty, William Palmer of Rugely, as the Judge was assuming the black cap and the warders closed round behind him in the dock—a custom with warders, lest the convict should attempt something violent or foolish—scribbled a note in pencil, and handed it down to his junior counsel.

"The riding did it."

Sir Hugo had not the strength of mind or nerve of William Palmer. He was perfectly aware that, somehow or other, the riding had done it. But he had not sufficient philosophy in him to acquiesce in the result. And his retreat from the interview was consequently not so dignified as it might have been.

Exit is the simple stage direction. But there are more modes of exit than one. And Sir Hugo, in stage parlance, did not go off as effectively as he could have wished.

END OF VOL. I.

www.ingramcontent.com/pod-product-compliance
Lightning Source LLC
Chambersburg PA
CBHW030641030726
47497CB00006B/1902